# METAL ANGELS

# PART THREE

# BY

# D K GIRL

**Metal Angels by Danielle K Girl**

Cover Design: Jake Clark
Editor: Inspired Ink Editing
ISBN-13: 978-1-7325368-2-1

To Mikie.

So close now. You watching?

# Kira - 38

Kira sighed into a platinum-coloured pillow, the satin smooth and warm against her face. Damn, it smelled good in here. Honey and spice and all things very, very nice. She should open her eyes. It was already bright in the room —she could tell from the dull glow against her eyelids—but her body lay in that blissful zone between sleep and wakefulness. Puffy-cloud floaty stuff, without the drugs. She rolled onto her back, and the satin sheet traced the curves of her body like a ghostly lover. All satin beneath her, too. Nice, but not great when things got hot and heavy. Nine out of every ten thrusts, you ended up sliding your ass right off the bed, landing in an inglorious wet pile on the floor.

Her hand slipped beneath the cover and found the warmth between her legs. She dragged languid fingertips over her belly, tracing a line around her belly button. Holy crap, she could do with someone else's fingers doing some work. Something to distract her. Her dreams had been bat-shit fucking crazy: Az going postal, the witches, the nearly dead kid wizard, and Facility assholes with attitude trying to rearrange her face with the grimalkin. Oh, and that chick, too. Nina of the great tits. *Where the hell did that part come from?* Sure, the sex had been mind-blowing, but it had been a long time ago.

The mattress shuddered. Someone who smelled of lavender and roses, and pretty, pretty things, joined her. Kira bit down on her bottom lip, squeezing her eyes shut tight. She wasn't exactly sure whose bed she'd ended up in, but that wasn't virgin territory, so why spoil the magic? Her body was a marshmallow. Fingertips ran a gentle line across Kira's brow, and she couldn't suppress a shiver. Butterfly kisses landed on her lips, and heat from a soft body pressed at her side. A brush against her flesh arm marked the pliable, unmistakable give of a breast, and she had the mildest sense of disappointment. Her sleep-addled brain had been pretending it was Eron leaning over her until that moment. He had a lot feminine charms, but tits weren't one of them. She really should open her eyes, but the darkness was soothing, and drowning in someone else's saliva might dissolve the echoes of that god-awful dream. Kira opened her mouth a little wider.

Her bedfellow obliged, their tongue working her own like a drunken slug. Kira groaned, pressing harder against the mouth that bore down on her, sucking then biting on the bulge of lip she found. Teeth clacked together, once then twice as the rhythm grew more frantic. Bodies shifted; a leg lifted and straddled Kira's hips. Nasties ground together, and the air filled with little yelps and moans. Kira's flesh hand found the swell of an ass that begged to be slapped. Two strikes later and it was getting hard to breathe. The woman edged farther down Kira's body, and strong hands pushed her legs apart, demanding access. Kira knew where this was going, and she kept her eyes tight as blinds. The tip of a wet tongue hit ground zero. Kira's back arched, and a choked laugh merged with a euphoric cry. She raked metal fingers down the back of the woman sucking the life out of her.

The armadillo was enjoying it every bit as much as Kira was. Warm, like she'd stuck it next to a heater. But on the very tip of the orgasmic precipice, Kira was left hanging. The woman moved, sliding her body against Kira's, snaking her way back up to mouth level. Kira battled through a bucketload of hair to find the woman's face. She didn't know where her strands ended and the other's began, and didn't give two fucks. Someone's hair caught at the edge of her mouth, stuck in the wetness there, but moving it would mean missing a second of the mouth wrestling. Not going to happen. Not until . . . and there it was. Fingers slid deep into the soaking wetness between her legs, and took all of two seconds to ring her bells.

'Oh god.' Kira bucked her hips. 'Oh fuck.'

The woman covering her, invading her, made her body jerk as if she'd touched a live wire. Vibrations ran through the metalwork of Kira's arm, all the way to where it had made itself at home up the side of her neck. A hand covered her mouth, and warmth spilled into her ear.

'Hush . . . they are going to think I'm trying to kill you, not help you.' Bemusement rubbed against the words.

Still knuckle deep, the woman sank onto the sheet beside Kira, cradling her close. Kira buried her face in hair and hard shoulder, gasping against the shudders that still tripped through her. Finally, after way too long, she was still. Then her eyes fluttered open.

Fuck. Kira braced against retreating fingers, then rolled away, turning her back on the woman lying at her side. 'How are you, Nina?'

A flicker of laughter. 'After that, much better now. Thank you, Kira. You?'

'Where am I?'

Her skin tingled at the feather touch of the sheet, and her bones were jelly. As much as she wanted to get up and storm out of the room, the reality was she'd just end up a sloppy wet mess on the floor beside the bed. Christ almighty, she was pathetic. You didn't forget a woman who smelled like the friggin' Garden of Eden. She'd suspected it was Nina the moment she'd awoken, but she'd still spread them. Or maybe it was *because* she'd known. Nina had always been a divine lay. Either way, still pathetic. And worst of all, Nina being here meant that messed up dream wasn't a dream at all. This shit was real, baby.

'In my bed. My home. Somewhere safe.'

Through the tangle of curls across her face, Kira stared at the view. But how the hell had she gotten here? Wherever it was, it looked like goddamn heaven. Sky as blue as the inside of a luxury pool, swathes of white cloud smeared across it. But it wasn't so heavenly across Kira's body. Aches and pains were beginning to surface, and the metal at the base of her neck pinched like a mother. Its heavy touch pressed on her ribcage, just above her right boob. Yep. The armadillo had grown. So much for dreaming.

Kira sat bolt upright. 'Vail. Where is the kid? Is he—'

She swung around, ass slipping on the damp sheet beneath her. Nina watched her with those doe eyes she had, a faint sheen of sweat on her brow. Her hair was a wild mess, framing a face that shone the way Kira remembered all too well.

'He is alive. Of course.' Nina rose from the bed, stretching her arms over her head and arching her back. Her locks flowed like a liquorice river down her back, and those glorious tits reached skyward. 'You still have a way to go before the Shift's effects fully wear off. Orgasms are great for the nausea, though. So, you're welcome. Would you like to take a shower with me?'

Hell, yes. 'No. I wouldn't. Jesus, what am I doing here?' Kira threw her jelly legs over the side of the bed. Ready or not, she needed to get out of this room. The moment her toes touched ground, she sucked in her breath. 'Shit.'

Glass. The massive bed, a California king, sat in an alcove made entirely of glass. Beneath her feet, a couple of hundred metres below, was a thin sliver of white sand and endless turquoise ocean, and to her right, a cliff side of reddish brown. Kira cradled her metal arm against her chest, suddenly feeling uncomfortably vulnerable. Totally exposed. Not just the wet clam but also the armadillo. She'd always covered it when she was banging Nina in Greece, had kind of hidden behind the faux skin somehow.

The shower hissed. Of course it wouldn't be in a private bathroom, like any normal shower should be. Nope. Not that kind of day. The shower was basically just a raised platform a few feet from the bed, completely open to the room and the daylight outside. Nina watched her, her hands sliding up and down her body. Water cascaded over honey curves.

'You are probably ravenous,' Nina said, a smile toying with the edges of her lips. 'You've been asleep for a long time. You won't remember, but I helped you to the bathroom earlier this morning. Tried to tempt you a little after that, but I couldn't get you interested in eating anything. Not even me.' She laughed and tilted her backside in a way that made the water dance off it.

Jesus. Kira had had blackouts before. Who hadn't? But her mind was a blank slate from when Nina had grabbed her, Az, and Vail in the paddock until this moment. 'What time is it?' She lifted the edge of the sheet and covered herself. 'How long have I been sleeping . . . wherever the hell we are?'

'It is about three in the afternoon, and this is definitely not hell.'

True. More likely it was somewhere on the northwest coast, if the red cedars clinging to the top of the cliff were anything to go by. The mere fact that they were near an ocean meant they were a friggin' long way from the farmhouse on top of the hill.

'Three in the afternoon?' It had been late afternoon when shit had hit the fan and she'd run into the Facility ass-wipes. 'But wasn't it—'

'Twenty-four hours have passed. Like I said, you've been sleeping for a long time.' The shower switched off, and a glistening Nina stepped from its confines.

'Twenty-four hours since . . .' Kira's words trailed off. Since we melted? Got roofied? 'Where is Az?'

Goddamn it, why couldn't she keep her eyes open? Her head was a bowling ball wobbling about on the top of her neck. Too heavy to keep upright. She lay back down against the pillows.

'Oh, the sun never strays far from his little star. Don't you worry. He's been checking on you with admirable regularity. Though he may have seen some things that will be difficult to erase

7

from his pretty little mind.' Tinkling glass shards of laughter filled the room.

Kira groaned, flopping onto her side like a whale trying to beach itself. Her metal arm hit the timber frame running around the edge of the bed, and the impact trembled all the way up to where the metal nudged at her neck. Ouch.

'You've drugged me.' At least, that's what Kira'd intended to say; it came out more like *Voo ugged maaa.*

'I saved your lovely, pert ass.' Nina leaned over her, hand pressed to the armadillo. Water dripped from her body onto Kira's own. 'Where exactly are you trying to go, Kira? You need to rest. And play. It will make you feel better, I promise.'

With an internal countdown, Kira marked three, two, one and barrel-rolled herself off the edge of the bed. For a second it was terrifying. Nothing but a pane of glass to stop her from plummeting to the ocean below. But the path to freedom was short. And the floor was fucking solid. Her back hit the glass with a resounding bang. 'Oh crap.'

'Now what?' Nina rested naked on her knees on the edge of the bed, coils of wet hair draped over her shoulders, strands wrapping around dark nipples. The view, admittedly, wasn't terrible. But it was hazy. Like a dust cloud had blown up when Kira had hit the floor. She blinked. Or tried to. Each movement dragged on way too long and did nothing to help her focus.

She gave her tongue another test run. 'What's happening to me?' slopped its way out.

Nina stepped off the bed and over Kira. Whoever she really was, she was still as big a fan of the Brazilian wax as she'd been when Kira had first met her. 'Your body is still adjusting to the Shift.' She crouched beside Kira and screwed up her face as she tried to get her arms beneath her. 'I haven't been able to Shift in almost a thousand years, and I dare say Enkidu may have given me more of a boost than I was ready for. You are not the only one feeling its effects.'

Enkidu. She'd just dropped Az's real name as if he were her best bud.

'Hart da wuk?' It was supposed to be a strong, concise *What the fuck?* And *How do you know Az's real name?* should have followed, but there was as much chance of getting that sort of cooperation from her mouth as there was of Nina getting her off the floor. Dangling mammaries were in danger of giving Kira a black eye, swinging low and hard as Nina tried to get some purchase. Waste of time. Even before the metal had gone all colonial and taken up more of her body, the Telteriun prosthetic would have challenged a weightlifter. It was another one of those weird things about the armadillo, though; she didn't feel the weight of it herself.

'This is useless.' Nina sat back, her hairless muff right in Kira's blurry line of sight. 'Odd, I don't recall the metal covering so much of your shoulder.'

Kira grunted, hoping it sounded remotely dismissive. Till she knew more about Nina than her favourite sexual position, Kira was staying mum.

Nina sighed. 'I'm going to need some assistance. Now, what is it you call him? Azrael?' She cupped her hands to her face. 'Azrael, mind giving us a hand? The little star has fallen out of orbit.'

Kira should have been worrying about important stuff, like why she was tired beyond belief and could barely see, and where the hell Vail was. Stuff that mattered. Nope. All she could think about was how bloody naked she was. And how the room stank of sex. And how much she didn't want Az to see her like this.

A panel of dark wood that camouflaged itself as part of the wall slid open. And though it was like looking through a sandstorm, the imposing silhouette was unmistakable.

'Kira.' Az ran towards her. At least, the blob that was Az did. 'What have you done, Ninshadur?'

He was pissed. Adorable. Kira wrinkled her nose. Take that, Nina. Or Ninshadur? What was with that?

'Nothing she did not enjoy, rest assured. Or is that the problem? Do I play with one you covet? A queen replaces a king for the wild man? I'd always taken you for a cock lover. I see I was mistaken.'

'You'd be wise, handmaiden, not to toy with me as you do the humans.'

Badass Az rumbled the words out, sending some serious burn Nina's way. But she wasn't far wrong. About Az loving cock, one in particular. He loved Gilgamesh the way Romeo loved Juliet. She'd seen it. Felt it, when Az had learned who he truly was. No broken human was ever going to fill that space. Nor did she want to. Everyone had a Gilgamesh.

Hers was slender, with eyes of white and hair like melted silver. Oh, for fuck's sake. What a shitty time for a deep and meaningful realisation. She loved that dumb-ass alien.

'I wouldn't dream of messing with you, my dear Enkidu,' Nina purred. 'I doubt I'd have the strength. And now that I've found you, I have no intention of losing you. I don't understand what you are doing here any more than you do. But you are the first trace of the gods I've seen in thousands of years. And I intend to learn why. I have a feeling you may be the chance I've been waiting for.'

Kira was fading. In all ways. Vision, hearing, general sense of existing at all. Almost a rerun of what had happened back in the paddock when Nina had grabbed them. Just as Kira gave up trying to fight it, Azrael lifted her from the floor. His hands touched her metal, and she spun off into a blissful black abyss.

## Blake - 39

Blake lay on her back in the chilled space, with little else to do but attempt to ignore the whispering in her head and contemplate just how far from her initial goals she had strayed. Instead of relishing the satisfaction of completing the carapaces, she lay hundreds of metres below the surface, tied to a petrified trunk inside a glass cage, being stared down by the animals carved into the ceiling. The splinter Tamas had jabbed beneath the skin at her right wrist like a needle for a drip—at least ten centimetres in length and thin as a needle—would not pull free, not matter how she scratched and tore and tugged. And the moment it entered her body, it were as if her contaminated blood had grown more laden with toxins.

The Waters that broke her down streamed through the glass surrounding her. All her joints ached, her nails ached, parts of her skin begged to be itched, but doing so brought no relief. She struggled to comprehend just what amount of time had passed since she'd used up Cym's offered syringe. Blake had stabbed the offered needle into her thigh moments before she'd been dragged to Tamas. Whether that had been an hour ago or a week ago, she struggled to comprehend. All she was certain of was that any positive effects of the last dose of medication had vanished the moment Tamas . . .

There it was. The conundrum. What had Tamas done to her? The innocuous piece of wood had slid so easily beneath her skin, but at its touch—indeed, at Tamas's touch—a piece of her core had shifted. Sunk away.

*Broken, broken. So very broken.*

Blake groaned, rolling onto her side. Of all the voices plaguing her, this one irked her the most. The whisper was far too close in tone and pitch to her father's. But he wasn't here. Could never be here. She knew that, as certainly as she knew her own name. A part of her burdened mind retained clarity; it was almost as sharp and focused as it had been when she'd taken those few sips of the Waters on that ill-advised day with Tamas, all those months ago. Granted, the bundle of synapses that still remained cohesive was slowly being dwarfed by firing neurons that created voices in her head. And signalled to her optic nerves that someone stood just outside the shrine walls. A shadow watching her. Unspeaking. Not answering when she called, but raising an arm every now and then, as though pounding on the glass.

Through half-closed eyes, she saw it even now. Hardly intimidating. None of the height of the Syranians, nor the stunted stature of Tamas. A stranger knocked on her prison. Sighing, Blake curled up into a tighter ball, hissing against the agony of movement. The dark spiderweb spread out from the barb of wood like veins and reached to her fingertips. In the sheen of the glass, the same veining was visible on her cheeks and across her forehead.

Exhaustion held her in a vice, and she was not so far gone she couldn't recognise the truth. She was not going to survive this. Somewhere along the line, as she'd shivered to the point of agony, she'd come to terms with that idea. A human body could endure only so much, and hers was making it clear that maximum tolerance had been reached. Aside from making her own erroneous choice with the Waters, she'd been violated twice by chemical warfare. Once with the truth serum, and then again when Tamas had . . . what had he taken from her when he'd clasped her head and fingered sheer agony into her skull?

What was he doing to her now? In this place?

*Breaks you. Breaks her. Found a hole inside you, and dug it deeper. Watched you both fall in.*

But she wasn't certain if what Tamas had done to her had *found* a hole, or built one itself. Bored its way into her programming.

14

Wrapped itself around her DNA. Tiny teeth gnashing at her undefined core. Blake recoiled from the memory, her empty stomach roiling. There were no words that could describe the sensation that had taken hold of her when Tamas had set that first poison on her and dragged from her the words she'd hidden deeper than her soul. But she couldn't let it remain nameless. Unknown. That was not how she moved through this world. Everything was ultimately knowable. And until the true name was known, Blake would call that poison the 'void-maker.'

*Pieces breaking, one by one.*

'Piss off.' Talking ignited fire in her throat, but she had come to understand her sister's affinity for cursing. There was nothing quite like cursing to centre one's self. 'Piss off, piss off, piss off.'

Blake curled her fingers into her bandaged fist. The Starpoints—those deceptively beautiful pieces of amethyst-coloured crystal that could bring down the entire Facility—shifted beneath her inflamed flesh, and a whole new level of pain radiated through her, flushing away the fuzziness and chasing back the whispers. The clarity lasted only a moment, but her mind reawakened each time she squeezed until spots appeared in her vision.

*Don't flatter yourself, you hardly fired the first shot.* That's what Tamas had told her, right before he'd ripped her apart.

Well, Tamas and his gods and his aliens could all piss off. When the moment was right, she would blow them back into whatever godforsaken galaxy or universe or dimension they had come from. And they could take their knowledge, their obscure metal, their toxic Water and superiority and utter disregard with them.

When the moment was right. And that was not here, at this altar. The Tier was where she must go.

Blake levelled a punch at the base of the trunk, a gnarled chunk the colour of old mould. Her attempt was pathetic; she was pathetic. So damn thirsty for everything Tamas and Captain Nex had offered, she'd not seen the forest for the trees. Her smile split dry lips, and blood oozed warm against her chin.

She was dying next to a tree. How insanely poetic.

Her cheeks ached, but this time from the ludicrous grin that would not fade.

Lifting her hand, Blake attempted to stretch one finger to poke at the wood, but her digits wouldn't play nice. And all at once her grin was the least ludicrous thing about her. She could not coordinate herself to move a few centimetres, yet she toyed with plans to leave here, move down several levels, gouge open her skin, and find the strength to activate the Starpoints.

It was quite possible she had already gone insane.

Flopping onto her back, Blake gasped at the bone-jarring impact and found herself staring into the eyes of the wolf on the ceiling. In some regards the carving was quite beautiful, certainly in comparison to the alien creature alongside it, with eyes wide as saucers on a body that resembled illustrations she'd seen of chimera, the monstrosities from Greek mythology. This creature had a thick-scaled tale but a body of fur, with curved hind legs like those of a horse, but the front end better resembled a bear. Blake did not know what the Syranians called the beast, and she had never asked. Fairy tales and folklore were not of interest. Kira had spoken of it once, but that conversation, as with so many, had not stayed with Blake.

'Would have been nice . . . to see her again . . . would have been nice . . . but not to be.'

At some point her mutterings took on a singsong rhythm. A true indicator of her diminishing capability. Blake despised singing of any kind. Christmas carols were at the top of the list.

'It can't be. Kira can't be here. They can't be here.'

A distant sound caught her ear. She allowed her head to loll to one side. The shadow stranger had not left her. The dark blob crouched low beyond the back wall of the shrine, both arms raised, waving madly. As she shifted onto her side and the Telteriun collar pinched at her skin, Blake winced but held her position. She blinked, as though that might wipe the stranger away. When it did not, she pressed her bandaged palm to the floor, leaning her full body weight against it. Red angry agony raced up from the wound into her shoulder, spilling down her spine, and a scream rose. But the shadow didn't fade.

'Not real.' The two simple words caught at the back of her throat, launching her lungs into hard spasms. Doubling over, Blake coughed at the ground. Blood speckled the emerald floor, the shimmering light from the moving water dancing against the stains.

## Eron- 40

Eron leaned his bare shoulder against the window. His sleep had been intermittent, despite Captain Nex's express command to rest so that Eron might render himself far less of a disappointment than he was apparently being. Brushing his hair over his shoulders, Eron touched his forehead to the glass and watched the specks of movement far below him. His eyes still stung from the effects of the contact lenses he'd removed at the first possible moment.

The sun was just beginning to slide down towards the high-rises but still emitted a blaze of heat and light. Its touch was a glorious thing across his barely clothed body. A pair of clinging black underpants was all he wore as he sought to escape the suffocating press of his armour for a little longer. The warmth caressed his skin like a hundred feathery brushes, his usually subdued nerve endings sparking with the contact. Agar's bullying use of the mea stone seemed to have heightened all sensation throughout Eron's body. The muscles attached to the stone ached with ruthless insistence, causing him to toss and turn most of the night. Added to this was the fact that despite the opulence of the apartment, no consideration had been given to the Syranian's height. Eron's bed barely contained his length, and he spent the night curled up in a tight ball.

Closing his eyes, Eron offered thanks to Cym. His brother was still tending to Gren at the Facility but monitored their vitals remotely. He had dictated that Eron should be rested, stating to the captain in no uncertain terms that his vitals were showing dangerously high levels of stress after three long days keeping Agar at heel. Eron showed the greatest signs of physical distress, but Parator, Seder, and Bel all struggled. Though Cym did not challenge the captain outright, his message was clear. The Syranians were being taxed too hard, too quickly. They may be hard to break, but it was not impossible. The god-soldiers must exercise caution, Cym warned their leader. Eron and his brothers were imbued with inordinate strength under Lord Lahar's blessing, but their god had not granted them immortality.

A short cough interrupted Eron's contemplation. He turned to see Clara standing just inside the door. Absorbed in his thoughts, Eron had not heard the door open.

'Eron, I hope you slept well.' Clara's eyes were bright under the blush of gold on her eyelids, and her gaze drifted languidly down the length of his body. 'My apologies for disturbing you.'

Considering she made no move to leave the room, the sentiment was clearly false. Her gaze rested just below his waist. The humans exhibited an inordinate amount of interest in what hung—or didn't— between his legs. And whatever Clara imagined hid there caused her blood-red lips to part. In truth, the Syranians shared little in common with the Earth gender they'd been assigned. There was no resemblance in genitalia at all, to either sex. No tubular piece of hanging flesh or delicate fold of soft flesh. His breath quickened, recalling in an uncontrollable wave of memory how those folds had felt against his fingertips, and against his tongue. The heat and dampness, the sound of Kira's voice when the roughness of his touch brought her release.

Shaking off the unbidden image, he glared at Clara, his temper flaring with increasing ease. 'Is there a purpose for your visit?'

Eron strode to the chair in the corner of the room, lifting the pair of trousers he'd discarded there at some inordinately early hour this morning. He'd worked all through the night with Agar, and the clothing stank of the nightclubs they had frequented. He turned his back on the gaping woman and covered himself, his movements brusque and jerky, jaw tight as his internal admonishment continued. Eron's gaze landed on the bag thrown into the corner of the room. A carryall with some essentials from the Facility – including an item he should have long ago destroyed.

'Yes. Yes, there is.' Her voice caught. 'There will be a debrief in fifteen minutes, in the lounge. Your presence is requested.'

Offering him a smile that Eron did not return, Clara backed out of the room. He entered the bathroom, swept his hair up into a bundled knot on top of his head, and splashed his face repeatedly with the ice-cold water pouring from the faucet. He shook his head, trying to dislodge his agitated thoughts.

*I fear for you, Eron,* Bel had told him in that sanctimonious way he had, *and what your failure to dissolve this attachment with the human may mean for us all.*

This was ridiculous. *Eron* was ridiculous. He proclaimed himself free of her, yet Kira filled his mind at the first lowering of his defences. Eron slammed his fists against the basin, and the entire vanity unit trembled. His temper was quicksilver, launching from him with far greater velocity than he was accustomed. Exhaustion, perhaps. But the darkness felt deeper, coming from his core.

*'Brandis mer.'* Eron kicked at the bathroom door as he strode out into the main room. 'You are a fool.'

He knelt beside the carryall he'd brought from the Facility, every joint protesting, and dug his hands through the bag's contents, searching for the device he'd never been able to bring himself to dispose of. A vestige of his weakness, Bel would declare.

Eron's fingers wrapped around the piece of tech, and he wrenched it free of the bag. A cell phone, unimpressive, black with faded numbers on the keys. Untraceable. Disposable. Kira had placed it in his hand months ago, when their deception had been discovered.

*The captain could go to hell,* she'd said. *Call me if you need me, Eron.*

Ironic words considering that very need had seen him banished to the lower levels of the Facility in the first place. He cradled the black plastic in his hand. Until little more than a week ago, it had never been used. But he'd never allowed its battery to deplete, had always kept it close. Like a talisman. Or a souvenir. The day after Blake had secreted Eron and Kira down to level eleven, to Azrael, the phone had rung for the very first time. Then again. And again. Kira had tried to contact him three times. And he'd ignored it every time.

*Call me if you need me.*

She had needed him. No easy admission for Kira. And Eron had thought himself steadfast and admirable for ignoring the call. He'd switched off the phone that day and buried it in his intimates drawer.

Now absolution and damnation rested in the palm of his hand. Bel was right. His attachment to Kira had not dissolved. The phone should have left his possession long ago. He should have reported Kira's attempt at contact the moment Azrael's disappearance had become known, advised them that she would not ignore his call.

Call me if you need me.

Eron had kept his silence. His secret.

Disgust rose, bitter and unkind, through his senses. All that for someone who had abandoned him. Opened herself to any who would have her. Left him buried with his mistake while she traversed the world. Yet he still clutched at the device the way a child holds fast to a favoured toy.

'Gather your senses,' he hissed at himself.

His redemption might lie in his hand. If he were to open the line, Kira may try again to reach him. A direct line to the woman both Tamas and the captain sought with a growing fervour. Eron's pulses flared, beating hard against the four corners of his chest. He curled his fingers around the device, unable to bring himself to activate it. Fury burned a coal in his depths.

'Are you ready?' Bel stood in the doorway. Eron jumped, dropping the phone back into the carryall. His room had become a frustrating hub of activity. 'Are you well, Eron?'

'Yes. I'm fine.' Eron drew on his jacket, kicking his carryall under the bed with as much finesse as he could manage.

Bel scrutinised him. And when he opened his mouth to speak, Eron shoved past him.

'Do not goad me, Bel. Let us go.'

He led the way down the hall and into the overdecorated lounge. Captain Nex stood by the plasma-screen TV. At the sight of his leader, Eron fought to subdue a snarl. Nex had pushed Eron to within an inch of his maximum capacity, had taunted him and belittled his ability to control Agar. An image rushed through Eron's thoughts: one of himself beating the captain into a bloodied pulp. The ferocious desire caught him off guard, and he pinched the bridge of his nose to gather himself. He must speak to Cym and request sleeping aids. Fatigue was setting Eron in a foul temper.

'The Messenger and I believe it prudent that you both view this footage. It was shot almost two days ago, captured by a grimalkin that was part of a team attempting to locate the stolen gallu . . . and the Lesser. The grimalkin was so badly damaged it was believed at first we had retained nothing of importance, but some footage of interest has been obtained.'

He jerked his chin towards Clara, and she lifted a remote towards the TV. Kira's face filled the screen. The image was jerky and pixelated, but there was little mistaking her features. Eron tightened his jaw and his resolve. Careful to make no outward signs of recognition. The audio was shockingly bad, barely discernible beneath the hiss of static and stutter of high-pitched electric squeals. Kira's dark curls were askew, her face dotted with cuts and darker marks that might be bruises or dirt from the roadside she sat on. The jeans she wore were ripped along one shin. Clearly, it had taken some effort to subdue her into the position they now saw. A blue car rested behind her. Her arms were pinned to it by the restraints originating from the grimalkin. She glared at whoever stood behind the mech, but her anger failed to mask her fear.

'The Lesser was located?' Bel asked.

The captain's gaze slid over Eron before it moved to Bel. 'A secondary team came across both her and the gallu on their way to another primary location. They were unable to initiate radio communications with the main unit, however. There was serious radio interference, which we believe now was instigated by the gallu somehow.'

Azrael causing radio interference? It begged a question, but just as Eron moved to ask it, the image on screen flickered and blurred, barely distinguishable.

'Pay attention, this is brief.' Captain Nex narrowed his eyes at the image, lips pressed in concentration.

Brief was perhaps an understatement. The footage drew into sharp focus, and snippets of Kira's voice reached them. She screamed, and a familiar repertoire of curses found their way through the static. Kira suddenly lunged forward, tearing the tentacle-like restraint from her shoulder and pulling hard, hard enough that the grimalkin hurtled towards her, the image bouncing with the mech's violent trajectory. The camera seemed unable to hold focus, and there was a blur of black and blue before all at once the mech was sailing through the air, spinning in tight rotation, then crumpling to a very definitive stop on the ground. Kira's lower body was still visible. She knelt on one knee, her metal fist pressed to the ground. It was difficult to make out, but someone was yelling at her. Presumably telling her to cease and desist. A few seconds later the screen went black, and Kira was gone.

'What was that?' Bel stepped closer. 'The Lesser did that?'

It certainly appeared so. But it could not be. The mechs weighed a veritable amount. It was inconceivable Kira could have just thrown one skyward. Eron realised he was holding his breath. He parted his lips, a side glance towards the captain telling him his heightened state had not been noticed.

'The Lesser could not possibly have instigated that kind of strength.' Nex shook his head, voicing Eron's own doubts. 'It is believed that the gallu must have been responsible in some way.'

'Azrael?' Eron said. 'I did not see any evidence of his presence.'

'But you will.' Captain Nex nodded at Clara. 'And his behaviour is not favourable to our mission. This is why you were instructed to view this footage. Azrael is no longer the subjugate you worked with in training.'

The screen lit up once more. Half of the image was too pixelated to discern, but the other half was all too clear. The image seemed to originate from a different angle than before. In this one the front half of the blue car was visible. Azrael strode away from it, wings pluming from his back, fine strands of metal glinting as he knelt down beside a human soldier, a young man. There was copious amounts of blood on the ground. Someone's booted foot was visible in the lower right corner of the screen. For the first time it struck Eron that Kira might not have survived this encounter. Was that her foot? Or would the captain force him to view her dead body? Eron's pulses were raucous, the pace of them making him dizzy.

Azrael leaned down, putting his mouth close to the man's ear. The movement shifted the spanning wings, and Eron caught a brief glimpse of Kira. Alive. Clutching at the car, eyes wide with panic.

'Ereshkigal has relinquished her hold on me,' Azrael shouted, gripping the man's shoulders.

More words followed, but they were utterly lost beneath a squeal of static. All at once, Azrael gripped the man's head in his hands; a moment later the soldier lay limp at his feet. The footage jumped, cutting out entirely before once again Azrael filled the screen. This time, though, he had his back to wherever the camera lay. He approached Kira.

Eron could feel the eyes around him. Weighty stares. Watching. His throat was a choked passageway. Breathing was impossible. If Nex forced Eron to endure this, then his imaginings of earlier – bloodying the captain senseless – would be realised. Anger snaked slow and deep at Eron's core, lifting its head.

Azrael's wings peeled back towards his body, offering a clear view of Kira.

She did not try to back away. Her eyes were fixed on the dead man. Her lips moved, but no words came through with the image.

Azrael reached for her. Eron leaned forward, his body coiled tight.

Kira didn't fight. But then, she didn't need to. The gallu did not attack her. He slipped his arms beneath her, lifting her from the ground. Kira wrapped her arm around him, exhibiting no hint of trepidation. She laid her head against Azrael's chest and closed her eyes. Eron dropped his gaze from the screen. Fierce heat snaked its way from a deep pit within him, feeding on the image playing over in Eron's mind.

The intimacy between Azrael and Kira needed no audio. No explanation. It radiated off the screen.

'He spoke the goddess's name.' Bel's concern did not reach his face, but it lay there in the undercurrent of his voice. 'I believed him to retain no memory at all of his origins.'

The captain folded his arms, still staring at the now blank screen. 'The gallu should have no recall of the goddess. Nor should the relationship between the gallu and the Lesser be possible. Yet we witness its existence. Both the gallu and the Lesser are still at large. We are interrogating a woman who was detained at the primary site. Tamas seeks guidance from the goddess, but She has not been forthcoming. Clearly, we must be vigilant. The situation has greatly changed. We cannot assume any longer that the Four will be unchallenged in this world.'

That sole fact was what should have concerned Eron most – that the mission that had taken his lifetime was threatened in any way. But his head felt fit to burst from the image it held. The torturous realisation that he'd been utterly abandoned. He curled his fingers into his palms, breathing into the sting that came when nails pierced flesh. The black screen, a taunting abyss, sat before him. It was all he could do not to tear one of his weapons from its holster and obliterate the mocking faceless panel entirely. The ache gripping him was nearly unbearable. So he sought the only release available to him.

'Captain,' Eron raised his chin so that he looked down on Nex, 'there is something I should tell you. I believe we may be able to utilise my relationship with the Lesser to our advantage.'

## Kira - 41

The real world slam-dunked itself all over Kira's senses. She jerked upright, her sister's name launching from her lips.

'Blake!' Her eyes opened to a blaze of light. 'Christ al-fucking-mighty.' Kira covered her face, blinking madly against the glare and sending the faint memories of another rough dream fluttering into the ether: Blake impaled on one of Az's steel feathers, her blood spraying from severed arteries.

Pretty stuff. Not scarred-for-life material at all.

Damn it, why was it so bright? And her hair was moving, lifting back off her face. Squinting, Kira stared up at a turquoise abyss. Little dark specks moved across the expanse, and for a second she braced. The memory of the drone rushing back in on her. One of the specks squawked, dropping down low. Seagull. Not a freaky Facility sentinel.

'Ah, there she is.' A liquid-silk voice came from close by. 'Does it remind you a little of the Mediterranean sky we used to gaze at?'

Shading her eyes, Kira turned towards the sound. The fluttering-hair thing was the wind. She was on a deck that jutted out into the air, ocean glistening for as far as the eye could see. Nina lay on a sun lounger beside her, clad in a shimmering gold bikini that was doing its very best to keep her assets in place. Right now was when Kira should be demanding to know where she was, where Vail and Az were. Instead, her eyes drifted down the length of Nina's body, a desert-gold sculpture of perfection, and her stomach did that clenching thing it did when something, or someone, turned her on. What the hell? Looking away, clenching her legs together, Kira nearly face-smacked the person crouching beside her.

'Oh fuck.' Kira jerked back. 'Az, what the hell?'

'He's been by your side for hours.' Nina sighed. 'You're lucky you were unconscious, though. He insisted on keeping the lights blazing all night.'

'Kira, be calm. You are safe.' Az's eyes didn't leave Kira as he spoke, droplets of jade she could bathe in.

Kira wiped at her lips, conscious of a damp patch of dribble at the corner of her mouth.

'I told you she would recover. Such little faith.' Nina draped an arm across her eyes, wiggling her hips as she settled. Her bikini bottoms were held together with bow-tied ribbons at each hip. The barest tug would have them sliding free. Kira bit the inside of her lip, cheeks heating. Seriously? Was this really the time?

'Do you feel any discomfort, Kira?' Az said. 'The handmaiden believed she could ease your discomfort from the Shift —'

'Ease my discomfort?'

'Orgasms should counter the travel sickness,' Nina declared, as if she'd just announced that oranges had a lot of vitamin C. No big deal. 'So I gave you as many as I could. Do you feel any nausea?'

'Jesus. No. I don't.' Kira tugged at the blanket that was draped over her. Someone had clothed her – plain white cotton panties, no bra, and an oversized white Adidas T-shirt. But she was still damp as the Amazon between her legs. And Az seemed to know exactly why. Normally, that would have been a huge turn on; messing with people was her speciality. But it was as if she suddenly had a brother, a really fucking old brother. And incest didn't make her to-do list. 'Can someone please tell me what is going on? How long was I out this time?'

'Only about twelve hours this time,' Nina said. 'I guess there was a little more punch in the Shift than I imagined.'

'I don't understand the words coming out of your mouth,' Kira said. 'What the hell is a Shift?'

Nina really needed to stop tracing her finger around her belly button. That was not playing fair. 'My preferred method of transportation. One I haven't been able to utilise for close to a thousand years. Funny how it just comes back to you, like riding a bike, as the humans say.' Nina's boobs jumped as she laughed, and Kira had to force herself to look away. 'As much as I do love to play with your body, I wasn't being entirely selfish. Orgasms keep the travel sickness away, a little perk I'd almost forgotten.'

Yeah. Okay. Right. Time to get out of this damn beautiful nuthouse. Kira pressed her hand against Az's shoulder. 'Dude, personal space. Can you back up a little? Is Vail okay?'

Before Az could answer, Nina replied, 'Well, he'd be better if he would let me touch him.' She smiled and waggled her fingers.

As much as Kira's hormones were Benedict Arnolding, they backed off for a second, and sheer pissed-offedness took their place. 'Don't touch the kid.'

'I didn't. Don't get your lovely knickers in a knot.' A long, exaggerated sigh came before a glint in her eye. 'But that large man-friend of yours is another story.'

'Large man?'

'Don't know his name, but he really was quite the ride. And I've always had a penchant for bald men.'

And here came the nausea. Nina had banged her, and Rossiter. Swallowing hard, Kira chased her thoughts back to the important stuff.

'Where is Vail? I want to see him. Right now.'

'Here, Kira. I'm okay.' The voice was little-field-mouse tiny and coming from a dark pile of blankets on the far side of Nina. Kira gazed across the swell of her breasts into a pair of solemn eyes nestled beneath a hood of blankets.

'Vail.' Kira threw off her blanket and leapt to her feet. 'You've been there all along?' The earth wobbled but she ignored it, racing to the kid with about as much grace as a patient coming out of anaesthetic. But she got there. 'Jesus, Vail. Buddy, oh wow. You look like shit.'

She crouched down beside him. Now it came back, crystal clear. The mess he'd been in when she'd found him. The coin was still embedded in his cheek, jagged skin around the edges a disgusting greyish green, and dark veins trailed out over his cheek. A couple crossed the bridge of his nose, a few more disappeared down his neck. 'Christ, does that hurt? Oh fuck, you were shot.'

Kind of a hard thing to forget, and yet her brain had ditched it till now. She tried to tug the blankets away from him, not entirely sure what she intended to do. Rip the kid's clothes off? But there had been blood, so much blood, when she'd found him. He put up a weak protest and she backed off.

'It's healing,' he said, giving her an equally weak smile. 'I don't think nursing is your thing, just saying.' He tried to laugh at his own joke and ended up coughing as if he smoked a pack a day.

'Comedy isn't yours, either. Just saying.' Kira took his hand, wanting to squeeze it. Say something profound. She was the adult here. Reassure the kid. Shit. She'd left him. What kind of asshole left a kid alone like that? This kind. The mute kind who couldn't find a way to say she was sorry.

'It's okay, Kira,' Vail said. 'We're good. I know you were scared. I'm just so glad you're all right.'

Oh fantastic. Now she felt like an even greater asshole. He was a wizard with a skill for mind reading. And forgiveness. One word, that's all she needed. Sorry. *Say it, bitch. Say it.*

'My arm . . . my fucking arm.' She stuttered like Tamas on a bad day, but kept her voice low. Close to his ear. 'The metal expanded and it went kind of Power Ranger on me back there, before Az beat the shit out of Tamas's goons.' She paused, breathing through the image of Az literally tearing those two soldiers apart. 'I don't know what the fuck is going on, Vail. And I'm so fucking scared right now.'

Look at her adulting. It was magnificent.

Vail's nostrils flared with a sharp intake of breath, and his eyes widened.

'What is it? Shit, Vail. You okay?' She grasped his hand. Vail nodded.

'God, you're pathetic. You're lying.'

Waves pounded against the beach below the wide wooden balcony, and seagulls batted  greetings at each other. A lot of people would pay a lot of dollars to sit here. But anywhere but here sounded perfect: Perry's stinking room above the pub, even Eron's shitty underground quarters. Eron. Oh man, what she wouldn't do to be pillow-talking with him right now. Back when things had been simple, she'd screwing an alien, and Blake had been building cages for ancient supernatural creatures. Those had been the good old days.

Vail lifted his head, almond eyes fixing on her. 'I'm scared too,' he whispered. In that moment it was just Kira and Vail. Nina and Az stayed silent as the dead behind them. 'I mean, I'm glad Nina saved me, but I don't know . . . there's something . . .' He rested his head back against the lounger, eyes fluttering closed. 'It's like something is trapped inside me. Every warding, every incantation, every working I know is holding back something . . . a void . . . a nothingness . . . I can't explain it. I wish Leona were here . . . and Bradley.'

'Me too, kid.' Now that was high on the list of things Kira had never expected to say. But goddamn it, what she wouldn't do to see the tan-queen disaster and Slimeball Sam right about now.

Or Blake. If only to slap her sister hard across the face and ask what in the name of all things fucking holy she had gotten them messed up in.

'Do you think they are okay?' Vail peered at her from his blanket cocoon, puppy-dog eyes fixed to maximum meltability.

This was it. Her moment to shine. Rainbows and promises of candy. Tell him yes.

Nina gate-crashed the moment. 'Were your witch friends at that farmhouse? The one on top of the hill?'

Kira shifted on her knees – the decking was sublime but hard as hell – and turned to face the destroyer of rainbows. Nina rested on her side, the sunlight catching on her raven-dark hair. Goddamn it. Down ovaries, down. This was getting ridiculous.

'Yep.'

'Truly? Well, that is intriguing. It would appear the dear old Wiccans grow in strength too, then.'

Vail tilted his chin. 'We're Disciples of the Maiden, descendants of the Wiccans.'

A sublime, fluid lift of shoulders, and Nina continued, 'Well, whatever you are, from what my assistants relayed back to me, I understand there was quite a bit of energy being thrown around up there. Those delightful people from the Facility actually reached the farmhouse before I did, which was actually what enabled me to reach you. They were so intent on the trace of preternatural radiation Enkidu set off at the farmhouse that they failed to notice the fainter trace nearby. I did not.'

'Great, well done. Your medal is on the way,' Kira said. 'What about the people at the farmhouse? Are they alive?'

Another lazy shrug. 'I have no idea, though Wiccans have always been rather challenged on the power scale, so it doesn't look good. But I was far too busy trying to cloak Enkidu's actual location. It is all rather exciting, I do have to say . After so long in a quiet world, to have all the supermundanes stirring again. I hardly remembered how to communicate with others, it's been that long. But to my credit, I rather quickly slipped back into old habits. Subjugated several lesser utukku, which was utterly refreshing, and useful. And it is all thanks to you, bright one.' She waved a hand over her shoulder towards Azrael. He stood at the railing, looking out over the diamond-shine ocean. He'd changed into a clean shirt, minus the bloodstains and shredded back. 'You and your shining star, with her divine parts.' Nina's eyes lowered to rest on Kira's metal arm.

Vail's breath hitched in his throat, and he kind of hiccupped his words. 'Do you think Leona is dead?'

Kira took his hand, squeezing it. Oh shit. If Leona wasn't dead, she was in some serious trouble. Words, find them. Use them. Be upbeat. 'Don't be stupid.'

'My money would be on the Facility. A place capable of raising and containing Enkidu is probably going to wipe the floor with a Wiccan.' Nina flicked her long dark curls over her shoulder, the move something out of a hair commercial.

'Will you shut your goddamn mouth?' Kira slammed her metal hand against the sun lounger, and Nina was jerked onto her back. 'She is not dead, okay. Not dead. Who the hell are you, exactly?' Az still gazed at the ocean. She grabbed at one of the pillows Nina lay against, ripping it free and hurling it at Azrael's back. Bullseye. Right in the back of the head. Not that you'd know it from his reaction. Concrete-wall steady. 'She knows who you are, Az. She used your real name. I heard you when I was roofied out of my brain. Thanks for that, by the way. Letting her fuck me over while I'm barely conscious—'

'You really are being quite ungrateful.' Nina's languid smile needed to be punched off her face. Or kissed.

Kira stood up, pressing her hand to her forehead. Shit, balls. Still horny? Seriously? She turned on Nina. 'Who the hell are you?' she shouted.

Azrael finally joined the party. 'Her true name is Ninshadur. She is a being of my time, although we have never met before now. We know each other by reputation only.'

'Your time?' Kira said. 'As in, the really, really long no-Maseratis time ago?' Jesus, how many of these ancient geriatric sons of bitches were here?

'Correct. I am currently immortal,' Nina said, much the way she'd say *Yes, I like nice clothes.* 'I lived, as did Enkidu, in a land called Sumer. I was a handmaiden to a powerful goddess who granted me the gift of immortality after I rescued Her from an undesirable fate.'

'Of course. How could I not have guessed?' Kira leaned against the glass railing, sucking in the sea air.

Az frowned. He was getting good at it. 'You knew this already?'

'She is using sarcasm to alleviate her stress, Enkidu,' Nina said. 'I knew there was something worth knowing about you, Kira, my little shining star. But I had no idea you would lead me to the sun. I mean, this is just . . . oh, gosh. There I go, tearing up.' She paused, and Kira turned to look at her. Nina was fluttering her hands in front of her face.

'You're crying? Why is there crying?' She raised her hands, looking to Vail. He was the insight wizard; he'd understand what the fuck was happening. He shrugged, his blanket fort rising and falling around him.

'I intend no harm, I can assure you, Kira. Were it not for you, and your imperfections, I would not be where I am now. With an opportunity I've sought for thousands of years.' Nina raised her knees, swaying them back and forth and giving Kira a view that was more than a little distracting. 'If anyone can understand my position, it is you. We share something in common. Unbearable loss. And we both crave escape, a desire to be rid of this world. I know how you came to have that arm. The pain of that loss eats at you, corrodes you, I see it in the way you treat yourself. Imagine thousands of years, thousands of losses, more than one of them like yours. My own mistake. You understand how unbearable that is.'

The balustrade was all that was keeping Kira on her feet. If the sun was still shining Kira didn't feel it. Her skin felt icy cold. This had gone real dark, real quick.

'Kira? Are you okay?' Vail sat up, even though it was clear the movement hurt him.

The seagulls were silent. Even the waves seemed to curl themselves onto the beach in quiet folds. Was she okay? Nah. Not so much. Nina had just torn her open and flopped Kira's guts onto the immaculately polished wooden decking, spilling a dark secret to the salty wind. Kira wished Blake and the ET's had never patched her back together again.

'That is enough, handmaiden.' Az's warning was a rumble from the centre of the Earth. A threatening roll of thunder.

But Nina's smile returned. 'Perhaps I was a little indelicate.' Perhaps. A chainsaw and vinegar would have been less painful. 'I'm not quite myself. It's been quite a momentous few days. What I wanted to say was thank you. For the opportunity you have led me to. The moment the gods left this realm, the preternatural energy began to evaporate. My mistress didn't warn me of that when I accepted Her gift of immortality. Not only would I live forever with my mistakes, I would be bored stupid. Human, for all intents and purposes.' Nina rose to her feet and sauntered over to stand beside Kira at the railing. 'I'll admit, I harbour a slight grudge towards Inanna in that regard. She was the goddess of war and fertility. Sex and violence were my lifeblood. We thrived on it. But She neglected to tell me that once She moved to the higher realms, all my lust would fade. I haven't even had a desire to start a bar fight, let alone a war, since she left. I was, quite frankly, rather pathetic. Until I took you into my bed, my little star. You feel it, even now. Don't you? The desire.'

Her finger swept along Kira's hand, wrapped tightly around the curved railing. This was where she should have told Nina to fuck off, but her throat was still too dry to talk. And as for lust, well, that had hit the high road like a Ferrari on speed. Which was actually a damn shame. Wanting to fuck was a damn sight better than wanting to die.

Azrael's shadow fell across them. He grasped Nina's hand and wrenched it from where it lay over Kira's. 'Stand back, Ninshadur. I will warn you only once. Release her from your influence. We may owe you the boy's life, but I will not hesitate to strike you down –'

Nina giggled. 'Oh, I don't doubt it, my little wild man.'

But Kira was still processing Nina's earlier words, and the penny was dropping in slow motion. 'Inanna,' Kira croaked. 'You were handmaiden to Inanna?'

The penny dropped for Vail, too. 'Oh my god.'

Inanna was a hard name to forget. Mostly because it was so close to 'banana', and Kira was juvenile like that. The sun warmed Kira's shoulders, and a breeze ruffled her hair. The world came back to life, and all the darkness Nina had stirred up drifted back down into the hole Kira was so adept at burying it in.

Inanna, the goddess of war and fertility. She'd read about Her in the back of Leona's blue shitbox. The goddess who'd

43

screwed over Her sister, tried to take her throne, and got Herself into all kinds of shit. Wow. Kira had never remembered so much trivial stuff in her life. But it was something else that bugged her. Something that hadn't come from the internet but from William and Miss 'I'm A Bitch For No Reason' Greta.

Azrael's boy King Gilgamesh had pissed off Inanna big time. Didn't want to screw Her, or something like that. And you didn't turn down the goddess of lust if you wanted to stay alive. Bad things happened to Azrael, to Enkidu, because his lover wouldn't fuck a goddess. Now, here they were, sunbathing with that very same goddess's old right-hand gal. For the icing on this weird-ass cake, whatever was going on in the Facility had something to do with Inanna's arch nemesis sister, Ereshkigal. The goddess who had supposedly signed Enkidu's death warrant, a very long time ago. The one Az had asked that poor son-of-a-bitch soldier about right before he'd torn the guy in half.

'This isn't good, is it?' Vail squeaked.

'I don't know what this is.' Kira watched Azrael, and he in turn watched Nina. 'Az? You all good with this?'

He didn't look good about it. Wait, scratch that. He looked fantastic, but his tense stance said he was as comfortable as a balloon in a dart factory.

'I am aware of who she was. But I was not about to let the handmaiden take you and the boy. Nor would I have left until you recovered.'

Nina stretched her arms over her head and declared to the wide-open ocean, 'I told you I intended no harm. Certainly not right now. I have no clue what game is being played. But it is truly wonderful. The gods breathe here once again, and I intend to find one so they can release me from this world.' She spun to face them, eyes bright. 'You are not dead, Enkidu, as you should be. Nor am I. It turns out we, too, have something in common. And that very fact could be the key to my freedom, and yours. If Ereshkigal is indeed behind this, if the goddess has covered up your death, believe me there is more than one deity who will want to know why.' She turned. 'But first, we eat. I make an incredible scrambled eggs. Who wants some?'

It was the mother of all segues. Yet in the scheme of things, it was the least bizarre thing to have happened in forever, not to mention mildly tempting.

But Vail shook his head and burrowed deeper into his blankets. 'I'm not hungry.' The shift of his body saw the sunlight catch on his face, and there was the very definite twinkle of tears.

'Well then pretend.' Kira tapped her finger against his thigh. Vail was more bone than boy. 'Get food into that gob of yours, 'cause I sure as hell am not taking the rap when Leona wants to know why you look like shit.'

Because they would see Leona again, and she would be in a state where she can talk and blame. Kira tucked the blankets in a little tighter around Vail.

Nina took her swaying hips and pert ass towards the doors, throwing a sly smile over her shoulder. 'Oh, Kira, I'm so surprised your career as a motivational speaker didn't pan out.'

Kira flipped her the bird and returned her attention to Vail.

But Az had his own two cents worth to add. 'I will remain outside,' he declared, resting on his elbows, continuing the ocean-gazing. 'I have no need for sustenance.'

Kira's stomach made it very clear where she stood on the need for sustenance and rumbled like a bowling alley. 'Well, you know what, screw you both. I'm starving, and I'm going to eat. And Vail, you are too, whether you like it or not. It's your lucky day; I'll be your waitress. Feel free to tip generously.'

Dry, chapped lips lifted, and the ghost of a smile brushed the kid's face. Bingo. Shortest game of bingo in history. The smile vaporised. 'We have to find them, Kira.'

'Yeah, I know, kiddo.' And she already had a long, willowy spaceman idea of how to do it. 'But first things first, I need to find some pants.'

# Eron 42

Eron manoeuvred the car into a vantage point down a narrow alleyway. His passenger had been silent for most of the forty-five-minute drive. Agar sat upright, back clear of the seat, as though at any moment he may throw open the door and hurl himself out of the vehicle. The gallu's heavy silence was at once both welcome and unsettling. Switching off the engine, Eron leaned against the steering wheel, only in part to afford him a better view. Exhaustion niggled at him, despite the enforced rest.

From their vantage point, there was a clear view of the main street. Just off to the right, two female police officers stood guard at a paltry blockade. A handful of dented signs declared the road closed. The midmorning air held sickening scents of melted plastic and charred wood. Directly ahead stood the blackened shell of what had once, a dangling sign declared, been an Indian restaurant. Kira's favoured food. Eron gripped the wheel, casting a sideways glance at Agar. No movement; the gallu might as well have been made of stone. If Agar sensed any of Eron's thoughts or dishevelled emotion, he did not make it evident.

Just as well, considering the cell phone had barely left Eron's mind from the moment he'd informed the captain of its existence yesterday afternoon. It had not left his person, either. The black device rested in one of his cargo-pants pockets. Switched on, volume set to maximum. But Eron's encompassing rage of jealousy had faded almost as quickly as it had begun and left in its wake a hollow sensation. If, by some unlikely odds, the phone were to ring, right at this moment, Eron was not entirely certain he would answer it.

*Why do you hesitate, Eron?*

The suddenness of Agar's intrusion in his mind almost caused Eron to jump. Almost. He'd grown more adept at hiding his reactions.

*Do you fear them?*

Agar's thoughts were never bereft of ridicule. Eron did not bother to answer the gallu's challenge, instead he narrowed in on the Bind, gripping Agar far tighter than necessary. But though Agar may be goading him, he was making no real attempt to wrestle control from Eron. The gallu's gaze feasted on his surrounds, prickling Eron's senses. He attempted to decipher the sensation. Pleasure? Bemusement? The exact label escaped him, but Eron understood enough. Agar liked what he saw. Drank it in.

The northeastern-most suburb of the city, an area called Montmercy, might once have been a beautiful place. The drive in had revealed a multitude of cafes and restaurants with lavish outdoor areas all along the main street, but as they'd travelled farther the opulence had begun to change. Fire had torn through great sections of the main street, leaving charred framework and melted store contents. At a minimum, shopfront windows had been smashed. The thick-trunked trees that were dotted at intervals along the road had not all escaped the violence, either. Some burned, most bore graffiti. One had an array of plastic chairs thrown into its ample branches. The place was a shadow of its former self, thanks to the violent riots that had taken place the night before.

Across the street, a couple of large black birds sat perched on a branch that had not been stripped of its foliage, like two tumorous growths as dark as the tree itself, heads tilting as they, too, surveyed the carnage. Rioting citizens had turned the area into something resembling a war zone. And it was not the only such place. The radiance being released by the Four had proved unfavourable to humans , the preternatural energy reducing the merely mortal to something base and coarse and igniting a hunger that coiled within and engulfed them.

49

At this rate, there would be little civilised about civilisation by the time they located Dumuzi.

*Why do we wait?*

Agar's patience, if it had existed at all, evaporated in a singular, sharp thought. He demanded passage to a hospital whose most direct path lay beyond the pathetic police barricade. Eron would get them there, but he would not do so with any urgency, suspecting this was no more than another attempt by the gallu to satiate his craving for pestilence.

'The hospital is easily walking distance from here.' Eron shifted the car into reverse, twisting to view the road behind. 'We will find a way around and go on foot.'

Agar exploited Eron's momentary distraction and stepped from the vehicle, easily finding his footing despite the backwards roll of the car. Eron cursed, choosing the choicest of Syranian and human expletives, and scrambled to undo his seatbelt. Agar strode with purpose towards the officers, forcing Eron to jog to catch up.

'This is a restricted area.' The taller of the two officers, a woman with curves and musculature suggestive of bodybuilding, raised her hands. 'There is no access here at the moment, too much structural damage.'

Agar's pace didn't slow, and Eron braced against the Bind. Fatigue pressed into the back of his skull with a formidable weight. The constant reining in of the gallu's power ate at Eron in small, incessant bites, and at this moment he did not wish to endure further discomfort for the sake of strangers.

'We simply wish to pass through.' Agar's voice dripped velvet.

'Hey, did you not hear me?' The officer's hand went to the gun at her hip. 'You're not going through there.'

The second officer, short of stature and hair, warded them back. 'Gentlemen, that is more than far enough.'

The pitch of their voices slewed through Eron's synapses, like knives thrown against his nerve endings. His legs worked before his brain followed. Eron broke into a run, aiming directly for her, before he or the officer registered what was occurring.

'Hey, back off. First warning.' The muscular officer barked the order, pulling her gun from its holster.

The command stabbed at something deep within Eron's mind. Too many orders were thrown his way. Day in, day out. He lunged, the pace so rapid the officer did not fire a shot before her wrists were tight in Eron's grip. He slammed the gun from her grasp, forcing her down onto her knees. Choked sound escaped her. Eron slipped one hand around her neck, finding a hold around the generous trunk there. Green eyes bulged, wide and panicked, beneath him. His irritation grew. He was disgusted at the spittle forming on her lips, the dribble of moisture from her nostrils. Eron's grip tightened, the stiffness of her windpipe evident against his palm. The humans were so fragile, so pathetically breakable. The officer gurgled, her head lolling forward and fluid spraying onto Eron's wrist. Iron disgust took hold of him. He lifted her as though she were no more than a mannequin and not the considerable lump of muscle and bone that she was. Her useless, delicate hands swiped at him, tried to claw her way to freedom. Eron brought her face to his knee, slamming bone against bone. And now there was blissful silence. Releasing her, Eron staggered back, struggling to catch his breath. A crimson veil of blood covered her mouth and chin, running in a torrent from her nose, which angled right with unnatural purpose. The sight set the pulses in Eron's extremities into a chaotic pattern. The mea stone burned ember-like against his bone.

Agar laughed, a hoarse and empty sound that only mimicked mirth. 'There is hope for you yet.' Velvet and venom were bedfellows in Agar's vocals. 'Shall we continue?'

He tilted his head. The second officer knelt at his feet. Her gun held to her own head, face white with fear. Veins bulged in her neck as though she struggled through some effort. Eron gripped the mea stone. The Bind was aflame, alive with energy. Agar's own. And Eron was ill-prepared for the agonising rush. He grunted, seeking to level his control over the Bind once again. The woman whimpered, her hand steady where it held the gun to her head, but the rest of her body shaking. Her fear might be her own, but the positioning of the gun was not.

'I could share this with you, you know.' Agar's meaty face twisted with what might be delight. 'Do you see how easily they are controlled?'

Eron could hardly ignore it. Nor could he ignore the rising heat that came with gazing on the human's raw horror. His throat tightened at the sight. Vibrations ran through the glands at his inner thighs and base of his spine, his sex ignited. Desire for domination spilled into every part of his sensory system.

'Please . . . no . . . no.' Tears spilled down the woman's face. 'Jesus, just stop.'

'Oh, Jesus isn't going to help you.' Agar's smile was so wide it threatened to split the skin in his cheeks. 'He was a mere mortal and died just as all you insipid beings will. Now, when I count to three, you are going to pull the trigger.'

Eron's focus on the Bind loosened, his gaze fixed on the woman. Agar controlled her, almost entirely. The mea stone's heat threaded through every vein of Eron's body. Each breath grew shorter and shorter with his hunger to see her finger push against the trigger.

'Three . . .' Agar's countdown ambled. 'Two . . .'

A sudden and raucous cry filled the air. Eron's attention thundered back to where he stood, his overbearing lust souring and grew bitter and wretched. He hauled on the Bind, using such force that Agar staggered. The searing heat drained back into the heart of the mea stone, leaving Eron hollow yet again. He tilted his head, searching out the source of the sound. One of the black birds swept low over them, screaming its protests. Agar levelled a blow at the Bind, and it was Eron's turn to stumble.

'No.' He gritted his teeth at Agar's resistance. 'This is not our purpose. Wipe this from her memories, and we will move on.'

Agar raged against him, as strong as an ocean wave against a shore. The officer let out a cry, slipping the gun nozzle from where it pressed to her temple to down underneath her jaw.

'Please help me,' she pleaded. 'Please.'

Eron cursed her inwardly. He was already watched with unbearable scrutiny for any sign of empathy towards the humans.

'Will you assist the poor, desperate woman, Eron?' Agar folded arms across his broad chest. The sun, hovering behind a lingering smoke haze, cast a sickly orange pallor over his features. And Eron saw it then, the truth of this matter. Certainly, Agar toyed with him, but it was also a test. One he could only pass with a show of utter disregard.

Let her die.

Agar's lopsided smile could be mistaken for a disfiguring scar. 'One.'

Eron's hesitation was infinitesimal, but it was there. He released his hold on the connection. Offered Agar free rein.

Nothing happened.

Tremors gripped the human's body, a dark stain between her legs betraying the loosening of her bladder. But no gunshot. The intense heat at the mea stone was extinguished, and the gun clattered from the woman's hand onto the road. She lurched forward, the contents of her stomach hurtling free. Agar slammed his fist into the side of her head, and her dreadful sounds ceased. The Bind hung loose, fluttering there for Eron to grasp and draw in.

*It is dull when you do not struggle. Are you broken in already, god-soldier? Am I to have no further amusement with you?*

The stench of vomit thickened the air, clogging Eron's nostrils. 'If they still live, you will erase their memories. We are done here.'

Eron turned away. His skin hung ill-fittingly upon his bones, that familiar hollowing seeming to have stolen the very flesh he was made of. Dampness clung to his brow. His pulses struggled to steady. He stepped over the body of the woman he'd attacked, keeping his gaze lifted from her bloodied face. Almost at the vehicle, he took a deep breath and turned to seek out Agar. The gallu had only followed so far. He stood on the sidewalk beyond the alley, eyes lifted to the sky. A flurry of darkened spots moved overhead. A flock now, all screeching their displeasure. The birds whirled to the left, banking in a circle, the entire flock in perfect unison, and dropped down low to the road, barely above the level of the low-rise buildings. They made a sure and steady path towards the barricade. Eron joined Agar, recoiling as the flock swept in a black curtain right by them. Each had a red patch of feathers around wide yellow eyes, beady eyes that fixed on Eron and Agar. On the tops of their heads, black feathers crested in a fan shape. Black parrots, perhaps. Eron had seen the creatures on one of the many documentaries he'd viewed while in confinement at the Facility. The animals of this world were truly beautiful, something he was reminded of as the flock banked again, this time to the right, but shifting higher once more. They drew upwards, black brush strokes against the grey-blue sky. Agar lifted his hands towards them, and the familiar tug jolted through the Bind. Nothing untoward, though, unlike earlier. Eron kept his eyes fixed on the flock.

A low crawling chuckle emerged from deep within Agar's carapace.

'What is it?' Eron shielded his eyes. After so many days of constant use, his contacts were like a film of acid across his corneas.

*We are being watched.*

Agar thrust his hands towards the fleeing birds. The mea stone throbbed, vibrating against the bone it fused with in Eron's arm. But he did not rein in the gallu. Mostly because he was curious to see what Agar did with the animal, partly because Eron's fatigue had returned with a vengeance after the gallu's display with the human. A great many of the birds fell from the sky, dropping as onyx bricks to the road and rooftops. A singular creature remained airborne, shrieking, then losing rhythm and dipping dangerously.

Agar lashed out again, but the creature eluded him, pushing higher with strong, steady beats.

*It does not wish to do my bidding.*

'What is it?' Eron hissed the question. Clearly it was not merely a bird, an airborne creature of Earth. Anything of bone and feather would have succumbed by now. Though, the creature was evidently distressed, rending the air with sounds like those it would make if it were poked with red-hot irons. Eron glanced around. The officers were unconscious and in plain view to anyone travelling up the road. The sounds of the terrorised creature alone would bring the attention of half the city. They were fools to remain here. The captain had informed them already that supermundanes were resurfacing since the arrival of the Four. This tiny creature did not warrant their delay.

'End this now, Agar.'

But Agar attempted to do just that. The swell of energy through the Bind told Eron as much. And yet the creature did not succumb. Eron allowed the barest slackening of his hold on the Bind, giving Agar greater rein. The gallu's thick shoulders bunched hard and high, every line and furrow on his face worked with mad intent. The bird dragged itself over the alleyway where the car awaited them, and Agar followed it. Not altogether steady, Eron noted.

*Release me.*

Agar's thought slid with a razor's sharpness through Eron's mind, and his concerns grew larger still. The bundle of black feathers fought Agar with astounding strength. The gallu had made some ground; Eron could just make out the splotch of red near the creature's black eye, but this tug of war was far from done. Eron pressed at the hexagons on the cuff, keying in the code that would vent the carapace and release the radiance. Rasping breaths broke from Agar, then he bellowed, head tilted back against the strain. His bare skin was illuminated with the faint spiderweb patterning of the release system. With the aid of the contacts, Eron followed the drift of golden tentacles up towards the creature taunting them. The radiance spiralled upwards, taking little time to reach the impact site, clasping around the bantam-sized catch. The gallu heaved back, like a fisherman hauling in an extraordinary catch. Now the creature's fatigue grew evident. Its wings hung down, the maddened flapping ceased, and its beak pointed down towards the alleyway as the radiance sucked it earthwards.

Eron brushed back a strand of silver hair that had escaped its bind. 'Is it dead?'

The words had not fully left his mouth when the answer became evident. Not dead. Very much alive. The speck of black bulged, feathers lifting in unison, bunching in a way that inflated the creature's size. Agar hissed, his features glowing with the radiance pouring from him. Eron blinked, fighting to understand what he was seeing. The bird's silhouette expanded, ballooned into something greater. Talons elongated and spindly legs lost their sheen of feathers, lengthening into spindly grey-skinned stalks. The black and red feathers, comparable in size to fingers on a hand a short time ago, now looked to be at least the length of Eron's arm, if not more. The head swelled into a shape more reminiscent of feline than fowl, a plume of feathers thick as a lion's mane, all in shades of crimson. A great beak hung like plates of armour from beneath bulbous eyes as dark as pitch. Paltry bird no more, this being rivalled the size of the industrial bins lined up along the alleyway.

*The true face of this beast is shown.*

Agar leaned forward, pressing his shoulders back before releasing a roar that dashed itself off the brickwork around them. The beast retaliated with a screeching bellow, certain to be heard from the next town over, not merely anyone nearby. Things had spiralled out of control with astonishing speed.

'Destroy it, Agar!' Eron shouted, dashing to the car.

He threw open the back passenger door and reached for the weaponry stashed in a stainless steel box resting there. He wrenched a haleon from its canister and pressed the device into the palm of his hand. Strands of metalwork wrapped around each of his narrow fingers, securing it in place. A tremendous weight hit the roof of the car, and Eron staggered back. The creature dug enormous claws into the reinforced roof, making light work of the metal. Giant sweeping wings arrowed towards Eron. He threw himself to the ground, rolling out of reach, squinting into the dust and ash stirred by the great wingspan.

'Agar!' Eron raised the haleon and took aim. 'Hold it steady.'

Flashes of red and blue ricocheted off the walls, reflecting in the windshield of the car.

Eron spun around. 'Shit.'

Two vehicles blocked the alleyway entrance, their occupants crouched behind them, guns pointed directly towards Eron and his strange companions. One of them shouted through a megaphone, but his words were swallowed up by the cacophony of noise levelled by Agar and the creature. Eron noted the horror on the faces of the men, understanding what it meant. There was a long list of supernaturals that the humans couldn't, or wouldn't, see. Luck wasn't with Eron today. They could see the beast just as readily as he did.

The creature's wings drove up and down, their tips raking the walls on either side of the alley, and one set of claws found their mark on Agar. They struck him, ripping great gashes in the faux skin covering one shoulder. Agar didn't flinch at the contact, holding fast to the flailing talons. The manic beating did little more than stir debris. Megaphone-man gave the order to shoot. Eron dove behind a hulking green industrial bin, pressing up against the brick wall. Rapid healing was a god-soldier asset, but that didn't mean bullets didn't burn like the Razinor Fires of Syrana. The officers fired. A shock pulsated through the mea stone and hit so hard Eron gagged, bile searing up his throat.

*Puerile fools.*

Other utterings flew from Agar's mind, acidic but untranslatable. Great gusts shifted the air. It wasn't difficult to source Agar's rage. The creature had bested him. Bested them both. It rose. Great wings hauled the massive body up into the air, moving the bulk with considerable speed. Agar's rage flooded through Eron. Fools had been made of them both. In a few wing strokes, it reached the rooftops, dipping out of view. Gunfire followed it all the way up. The raucous sound was magnified in the narrow alley. Eron lashed out with the Bind, landing deep claws into Agar's psyche. He disconnected the vent system, punching in the code with trembling fingers. Agar's glow vanished with a sudden snap, the disconnection hunching him forward, but his fury was unabated. Eron sank into it, let it feed into his own.

Again, the humans had meddled where they ought not, causing a distraction that had cost them the creature. Once again these people had interfered in his life. In his purpose. Eron's anger rose up and over Agar's own and encompassed them both.

*Let them know your displeasure, Eron. Make them see.*

Eron raised his arm towards the police vehicles. The haleon— a sheath of metal against the palm of his hand — shimmered with diamond points of light. Eron released the firepower, letting the heat of his anger flow with it. A shock wave pulsed towards the officers. Both they and their vehicles were lifted and catapulted backwards in a shower of broken glass. They crashed into the front of the scorched shops on the far side of the road. Breathing hard and fast, pulses thundering, Eron decided more could be done. With a change of mode on the haleon through a flick of his wrist, the fuel in the cars' tanks ignited. A roaring gush of flame erupted from the crumpled piles of metal. The heat slammed against him, and Eron threw his head back, relishing the burn against his skin. Skin that felt barely able to contain the wildness within. He longed to tear it from his bones, strip back the layers and lay bare his core. Once again, the glands of his sex throbbed at the base of his spine, the ache of tiresome suppression threatening to tear open the muscles that contained them. The sudden craving engulfed him. Her silhouette filled his thoughts, larger than any life around him. Her scent against his nostrils, his tongue against her wetness. In that moment he knew he would tear the world in two to be with her. Abandon his purpose. Abandon his god.

No.

Eron jerked his head forward, struggling to catch his breath. He'd given her up. Suppressed his desire. For Lahar. The sacrifice had been made. Blinking away the image of Kira's nakedness, Eron sought out Agar. The gallu stood silent, face devoid of any expression, but something lingered in the fathomless pits of his eyes. A tangible, alluring thing. Just as it had been in the Facility, the day Eron had Bound with him. The creature encroached further and further each day, darkening Eron's world.

He reached for the mea stone, pressing his hand down hard on the solid lump in his arm as he sought physical contact, a connection with the world he stood in. His reality. The one where Kira was no longer his. The fog lifted and sent the crawl of darkness back to where it lurked deep in Agar's eyes. The damage inflicted by both weaponary and flying creature upon the gallu was extensive; strips of faux flesh hung loose, exposing the metal beneath, but Agar's serpentine smile did not falter.

'We are done here.' Eron turned his back on his tormentor, and the abyss of his gaze.

## Kira - 43

Kira and Vail lay on a burgundy couch apparently constructed to hold a family of eight. Eight basketball players. Every seat was a chaise, and the ottoman was the size of a kid's wading pool. Luckily, the room was about double the size of her apartment at the Facility, so there was no problem. Well, no problem except you needed a certain level of fitness to manoeuvre yourself back into the forest of cushions, which had set up a breeding ground on the massive couch. Kira stretched her arms overhead, trying to stop the muscles between her shoulder blades from punishing her for carrying Vail in from the veranda to the bathroom a couple of times, then finally setting him here, tucked up in the far right corner of the couch.

'You sure you're good? It looks like I broke your neck.' Kira would have nudged him with her foot, but she wasn't remotely close to where Vail lay in a lopsided huddle, even with her legs stretched out the length of the couch. 'Probably not the best position, considering . . .'

Considering he'd managed two mouthfuls of Nina's admittedly jaw-droppingly good scrambled eggs before he'd started retching. Poor bastard had been mortified, and credit to Nina, she hadn't lost it when her blush-pink cashmere blanket had taken the brunt of the projectile. She'd cleaned it up herself, a pair of lilac gloves covering her perfect manicure. Maybe when you were immortal, you got used to shit like that.

'I'm not feeling sick, and I'm very comfortable, thank you.' Vail peered at her from beneath his blanket hoodie. The kid shivered, no matter how many of the bloody things she piled on him. 'Honest. I'm just into this movie.'

'No one is into this fucking movie, not even the actors.'

'Harsh.'

'Delivering the truth, my friend.'

The TV – bigger even than the monstrosity in the hotel room back at Beleiro – was switched on, though it would have been more entertaining to watch the wall behind it. The midafternoon movie on a Wednesday (and she only knew what day it was because a midmovie news update had told her so) was sickeningly bad. Who gave a shit about some kid's dog running away? And for the love of god, how was it possible that Nina had no internet access here, so they could watch something bearable? Or, better yet, find out where the fuck they were. Or if the Facility was still standing? Kira smelled bullshit, thick and pungent. Actually, she smelled garlic and coriander, the leftover waft of the scrambled egg feast from hours ago. Fuck. That last espresso was a mistake. Kira was going to shake her legs right out of their hip joints, or, at the very least, tear the fabric of the black silk pants Nina had given her to wear, if she didn't stop jigging. The fabric was so light it felt as if Kira wore nothing below her T-shirt at all. Buzzed as she was, Kira's eyes didn't leave Vail. She didn't like the way he kept pressing his lips together, eyes steadfastly locked on the screen.

Mercifully, the movie cut to an ad break. Vail sighed and shifted. His blanket cocoon twisted around him, and he let out a small gasp.

'I've got this.' Kira launched herself across the vastness of the couch desert, snatching up the bright red bucket that rested on the lagoon-sized ottoman. 'Bucket in three, two –'

'I'm not going to be sick, Kira.' His smile bunched up the skin around the coin embedded in his cheek, but his eyes were bright enough, and the giggle sounded genuine. Operation No-puke was abandoned. Kira slumped back against the cushion forest, resisting the urge to dig her fingers into the groove between metal and flesh at the base of her neck. Christ it was uncomfortable, both the metal itself and thinking about why the fuck the armadillo had spread at all. So damn uncomfortable she was in full denial mode. Think about all the other shit going on. And, damn, there was plenty of it.

'How's your . . .' Kira waved a finger towards Vail's torso.

'Gunshot wound?'

Kira nodded.

Another smile appeared. 'Well, I don't know exactly what Nina did to me, but I can barely feel it.'

A thought had bugged her from the moment Nina had mentioned travel sickness and orgasms. She chewed at her lip a second longer before asking the question. 'Hey, Nina didn't . . . after we Shifted, did she touch . . .'

'Touch what?'

Could his eyes get any rounder?

'Your dick, did she try to touch it? Did you and Nina —'

Vail's eyes *could* open wider. He threw back his head, the blanket hood sliding free, and let loose with a high-pitched giggle. 'Gross! No way.'

Okay, mildly insulting, but the kid apparently wasn't tent-poling after the Shift. Unlike Kira, who was still feeling the edge even now. And that didn't sit well. She fucked when and whom she wanted, that was her thing. Her slice of control. But she didn't trust that that control existed right now. When Nina had headed back to bed after brunch, and *didn't* invite her, Kira had been way too disappointed. Way too tempted to start following her down the hallway.

She wriggled to the edge of her seat, the lace panties Nina had given her taking refuge in her ass crack. 'Why the hell is that gross?'

The kid snorted, actually snorted with laughter. 'Oh man, okay, now I'm uncomfortable.'

Uncomfortable maybe, but still amused. Weird, really. The buzz it gave her to hear his laughter. No matter what an ass she was being, the kid found her amusing. He looked at Kira as if she were a rock star. She'd abandoned the scrawny bastard in a paddock, run away from him like a lemming on speed, yet the sun continued to shine out of her ass. The idea she was anyone's rock star gave her a weird set of feels. Kira got to her feet, deciding to go bug someone who would be reliably unimpressed by her. 'I'm going to go check on Rossiter.' Again. 'You be okay here for a second on your own?'

'I'm not going anywhere.' Vail yawned.

A newsreader's head filled the giant screen. Hell of a lot more appetising to look at than a mutt. The dude had honey-brown eyes, a shade that reminded Kira of the contacts Eron preferred. The idea that had come to her before she'd stuffed herself stupid, the really totally stupid idea about trying to contact Eron, still sat there humming at her.

*It's the dumbest fucking idea you've ever had. Nina's got you all stirred up. Think straight, dumb cow.*

Kira tapped her knuckles against her neck, where the armadillo had stopped its northward migration just below her right ear. Vail mightn't have an appetite, but hers more than made up for it. She'd wolfed down the eggs and toast as though she'd been starved half her fucking life. Maybe that's what happened when you went all Bionic Woman. She'd hurled a goddamn grimalkin as if it were a plush toy. What the fuck was with that? And how much higher did the armadillo intend to go? 'Cause it was a pretty safe bet this metal wasn't see-through. If it headed farther north, anywhere near her eyes and nose, she was going to lose her shit.

The guy on the TV, Peter something, was still talking, harping on about rioting in a midstate city —New Weston—and how authorities were considering curfews in some suburbs to combat the violence.

'The reasons for the upheaval have yet to be determined. Hospitals in the west of the city are struggling to cope, as the riots come alongside an outbreak of a flu-like virus that has seen a spike in transmissions. There are new reports that a similar situation is coming to light in Telbourne, just seventy kilometres from New Weston. We will bring you updates as we receive them.'

The good citizens of New Weston were restless and coughing up lungs. Good to know she wasn't the only one having a bad day.

Leaving Vail to learn the fate of the fleabag, Kira made her way into the bedroom where Rossiter still lay dead to the world. It hadn't been Kira's imagination as Nina had rushed them out of the field and away from the carnage Azrael had created on the road. Rossiter had called to her, her ears hadn't deceived her, even as the world had melted away around them. Nina had gone back for him, but doing it without Az seemed to mean Rossiter's 'travel sickness' was heavier than anyone else's – despite Nina's most rigorous use of her unique 'remedy'. A remedy Kira couldn't think about too much right now.

'Yo, Ross-man.' Kira leaned down, speaking right into his ear, and none too quietly. 'Speak to me, baby. Our immortal lay does not lie about one thing. She makes a fucking mean scrambled eggs. Saved you some. Cold as shit by now, but her microwave looks like it could power a small city.'

The human tree trunk rolled over, nearly decapitating her with a swinging arm, and burrowed down deeper into the snow-white coverings. The quilt cover had Japanese lettering stitched into it in some sparkly gold thread. It offset his brown skin nicely. Kira tapped Rossiter's head. The huge noggin might as well have been a rock. She sighed, her foot doing Morse code against the base of the bed. She'd hit the espresso machine too hard. The mess her nerves were in had quadrupled with that last shot of Kenyan. Now her flesh fingers shook as if her brain were malfunctioning. Which, maybe it was.

She picked up Rossiter's trousers for the third time in an hour, as if somehow the cell phone she wished was there would magically appear. It didn't. Nor did it appear in any of the drawers in the room or the empty cupboard. Or under the bed —another California king—or even under the bedcovers. Now there was a view she wouldn't be forgetting anytime soon. Mount Fuji was hiding out under the R-man's Y-fronts . Nina must be a happy girl. Kira padded over to the window but couldn't see any sign of Az. He'd been propping up the balcony railing for a while, but she got the sense he was as restless as she was. Not through any hoodoo-voodoo connection, just by the way he stared out over the ocean as though he were willing it to rise up and wash him away. Kira breathed against the glass. This place was mostly glass, when it came down to it. A beautiful goldfish bowl. Couldn't have been more different to the prison-camp Facility if it were trying. Kira drew a smiley face in the condensation. Jesus. She almost missed that prison camp. Blake. Eron. Kira wiped her metal hand across her artwork, contact with the glass setting off a screech that a banshee would be proud of. Kira glanced once more at Rossiter. Dead to the world.

She left him to his dreams, but she wasn't in the mood for watching kids sob over their long-lost shit-sniffers, so she headed down the length of the hall, past the random bedrooms and a gym that she'd already sussed out. They already knew for a fact that Nina didn't just Shift everywhere. She'd been in the Maserati the first time they'd come into contact. There had to be a garage here somewhere. She reached the door at the end of the hall. It was glass; hell, what wasn't in this place? A set of black marble stairs led down into the underbelly of the house. Door was unlocked, as all the house seemed to be. They didn't appear to be prisoners, but who knew? Nina was some handmaiden to a goddess, an immortal being who could transport them from one point on Earth to another. She could probably click her fingers and melt organs, or turn them all into dribbling sex slaves. Why the hell would she need a lock on her front door?

Kira moved down the flight of stairs and into what could be, if you had an icemaker, a small skating rink. It was, in fact, a garage. Housing several Maseratis. Sensor lights reacted to her presence and illuminated the vehicles. One white, one British racing green, both gleaming as though they had glitter embedded in their paint. The cars enjoyed a perfect view of the ocean through floor-to-ceiling windows. 'Cause that's what your four-wheeled friends needed, right? Ocean views. Jesus Christ. Kira edged around the white Maserati, trying to peer into its interior, but the tint job was heavy. She tried the handle, and the door opened with an expensive-sounding silence . The heady odour of fresh dead cow skin wafted free. Not a speck of dirt on the floor mat beneath the steering wheel. Nothing to show the car had ever been driven at all.

But as nice as the car was and all, sans the dead cow, the best thing about it was the rectangle of black propped on the dashboard.

'Oh fucking bingo.' Kira slid into the driver's seat and reached for the cell phone, tugging it free of its cradle. She pressed the power button, all the while giving herself a stern telling-off.

Bad idea. This was such a bad idea. Kira sent up a silent prayer to whichever god wasn't fucking with her that the phone would need a passcode, a fingerprint, something that would stop her from dialling the number.

A touch to the screen and all at once she was Eve, standing butt naked in the Garden of Eden with the ripest, juiciest apple gripped in her hand.

'Shit, balls, shit.' The keypad glared up at her, taunting her. 'Oh fuckity fucksticks.'

Blame the hormones. Or the almost dying. Vail almost dying. Blame Blake sending her out here to begin with. Hell, blame Captain Nex for being an asshole to begin with. If he'd just let Eron fuck around, live a little, Kira wouldn't have had to sneak him out of the Facility. Wouldn't have been so damn good at it her sister had gone on to send her on some suicide mission with an ancient dead guy.

Damn it. Number dialled. Phone pressed to ear. Stomach contents doing a performance Cirque would be proud of.

Three rings and she was out. Okay, four. Wait, no let's go for an even ten.

Connection. Right about now, a regular heart would be banging a heavy-metal tune against her ribcage. Eron had kept the phone. Despite getting his ass whooped, he'd kept the fucking phone.

'Eron?'

If he didn't say something, the caffeine was going to shake her apart.

'Kira.' Flat as a pancake. So much for a breathless, desperate sound of recognition. The silence was deafening.

'Hey, Eron . . .'

'Why are you calling?'

Nice to speak to you too, Eron. 'Oh you know, just wanted to say hi. How's things?' She toyed with a windshield wiper , flicking it against the glass.

'They have been searching for you. They want Azrael returned.'

She chewed at her bottom lip. Right. So much for a heartfelt *How are you? I miss you.* Yep. Dumb idea.

'Eron . . . I don't know where he is. I mean, yeah, I was with him initially, but he ditched me long ago. I fucked up, I get that. But I'm on my own out here now. The guy can fly, did you know that?'

A soft grunt, the sound of movement. She closed her eyes, picturing him. Limbs of snow that moved like a dance. That stupidly pouty mouth. The smile. Christ.

'I'm aware of his capabilities.' A sigh. 'Are you all right, Kira?'

And cue the mushy insides. Happy juice cascaded through her body. Pathetic? Yeah, just a little. 'I'm . . . yeah. I'm doing okay. Are you?'

'Yes. I am well.' A tremor, so faint she nearly missed it. But they'd spent too many nights face-to-face talking shit till they were both drained for her not to catch the slight alteration. Her happy juice ran dry. Warning bells were ringing, or maybe that was the eggs. Either way, she didn't feel so good.

'Blake,' Kira blurted out. 'Is Blake okay?'

Nothing. Barely even the whisper of breathing.

'Eron, please tell—'

A sharp sound, maybe static, or if she let her imagination go wild, Eron catching his breath. 'Where are you, Kira?'

'Good question—'

'Kira, this is truly not the time.'

There it was again. Was he coming down with a cold or something? The guy sounded choked up.

'Time for what?' she said.

'We've seen what Azrael did, the deaths he caused. By continuing to—'

'I told you I don't know where he is.'

'You're lying, Kira!' Eron shouted down the line. The dude barely raised his voice when he came, but this had him all riled up. 'I've seen the footage. You went with him willingly, he protected you. Now tell us where Azrael is.'

Kira hung up and threw the phone across the garage. It slammed against the glass, and the battery separated from the main unit. 'Asshole, fucking asshole.' And she was a stupid fucking dumbass moron.

Tell *us* where Azrael is? Us. Did she really think her pussy was that fucking mesmerising she had Eron nailed for life? Yes. Yes, she did. And holy Christ on a cracker had she been wrong. Kira ran to the phone and tore the SIM card free. It needed to go in a microwave or something. Melt it. That's how you stopped people from tracing a call, right? Fuck. Shit. Balls in a pizza oven. Had he been trying to trace it? Eron sounded pissed as hell. Like he wanted to tear her a new one. Eron. Mr Sugar and spice and all things nice.

She blinked. Fucking dusty down here. Eyes watering.

A muffled scream reached her. Someone pounded against a door.

'What the—' But she knew what before the words could finish forming. His terror swept through her, notched up her trembling fivefold. Azrael. Close by. And shitting his pants. 'Az? Where are you?'

Kira followed the thumping, a manic beat against a hard surface. She raced down the only other corridor leading out of the garage. A concrete hallway that led to another flight of stairs. A spiral staircase leading down into the depths. Somewhere in those depths, glass shattered. Seriously, this day was in contention for worst ever.

'Az? Are you down there?' The wash of panic coming from him made it hard to negotiate the narrow staircase. Kira bounced off the railing and nearly tripped over her own feet twice. 'Holy shit, Az.'

She jumped the last step, hitting solid ground. Kira trailed her hands along the walls, metal fingertips grinding against the hard surface. Christ almighty, if Az didn't calm the fuck down, she was going to have an aneurysm. Or shit herself. Fear was peeling them both wide open. It took every ounce of control not to drop to her knees, curl up in a ball, and choke on the panic.

*Dark. Dark.*

The word came to her over and over, an automated message stuck on a loop. But it wasn't dark. Not where she was. The lights sensed her movement and blazed a path ahead of her. Finally, three stainless steel doors loomed. The selection process took all of two seconds. The door on the right. The one that was shuddering with the weight of Az's body hurling against it. And it was his whole body. The blows ghosted through her own, the armadillo vibrating with each desperate launch he made. Kira grasped the silver handle. Unlocked. She wrenched it open. The unmistakable scent of wine, deep and rich, rushed into the hallway. Az hurtled out, but his wings were at full expansion. Their razor edges dug into the frame and lodged him there. Az's cries grew more frantic, his terror building into a monstrous thing. Any second now Kira would be doing a Vail, hurling her guts all over the place. This was raw stuff, like watching the scariest movie of all time, all alone, and hearing someone outside the window.

'Az, buddy, calm down. It's me .' Red wine bloodied the floor, seeping around their feet. Az's bare feet skidded on the wet surface. 'It's Kira. Hey!'

Shit, he was going to tear himself apart. And he was taking bits of her with him. Kira flexed her fingers and raised her arm. 'Don't take this personally, Az.'

If he did, chances were she'd become a human shish kebab. Kira slapped an open metal palm to the side of his face. Az's head slammed against the door frame, bouncing off the hard surface. But Kira wasn't about to become a Middle Eastern delicacy. Not today. Azrael slumped, silent, pinned by his own wings in the doorway, hair a mess over his face.

Holy shit. That had been the mother of all freak-outs. Head and shoulders above anything she'd experienced with him before. Enkidu was just as scared of the dark as Azrael had ever been.

'Az?' Kira edged back – as if she had any hope of outrunning him if he went for her. But her skin had stopped crawling, and her bowels were no longer trying to dump a load.

'Kira.' Az raised his head, and his eyes found her. 'There was such darkness, emptiness. I could not escape.'

The guy looked like he'd just gone three rounds with a team of heavyweight boxers. It was not the time to tell him the door hadn't been locked.

Kira moved in closer but didn't touch him. The fever-pitch panic might be gone, but the undercurrent was still there. One touch of metal to metal and she wasn't sure he wouldn't go through the roof.

'What were you doing in there, Az?'

He tilted his shoulders, and the left wing gave up its death grip on the door frame. 'Wine. It calms you. I sought to bring some to you. The handmaiden had shown me this location whilst you slept.'

'You were getting me some wine?' Potential aneurysm be damned. A dude who was deathly afraid of the dark had come down into the cellar to get her a bottle of shiraz. It was quite possibly the nicest thing anyone had done for her. A nice contrast to being screamed at by your alien lover.

A thank-you was on the tip of her tongue, but Azrael wrenched his right wing free and stepped up close. Super close. Nose-to-nose type stuff, if Kira were taller. Right now it was kind of nose to sternum.

'I cannot return there, Kira.' Jade lasers bored into her. As if he were still searching for somewhere to hide.

The fear bubbled low and quiet, a big vat of stewy muck in that hollowed-out place they shared.

'To the cellar?' Stupid fucking thing to say. She knew full well he wasn't talking about the cellar, but this scary movie needed to end. Right now.

'Kur. Where Ereshkigal kept me . . .' Wherever the big-titted bitch kept him had been bad enough to reduce him to a trembling mess. The Telteriun angel was rattling in his metal cage. 'I cannot return to that darkness, Kira.'

Screw the no-touchy-feely thing. Kira pressed her hands to his face. 'Hey, Az. You're not going back, okay? It's going to –' Whoa. Okay. This was nice. Zen time. A hot bath and a glass of wine, chill. Was she still breathing? Didn't matter. This buzz gave her – them – all they needed. Az's eyes stopped doing their crazy dance across her face and found her. She dove right in. 'You're not going back. It's not going to happen. I promise. Blake owes me big time. And she'll find a way. That goddess can go fuck Herself if She thinks She gets you back.'

Kira'd kill that motherfucking deity with her bare hands if need be. Who did that divine cow think She was? People had a right to be forgiven, for fuck's sake. People made mistakes. All the time. Stupid, senseless mistakes. And—Kira could vouch—they would take them back in a heartbeat.

If they had a heartbeat.

She let out a slow breath, the press of metal over her boob helping to push it from her lungs. Not a freaky thing, but oddly comforting. Almost a gentle hand on her shoulder. Jesus, this day was long. Her fingers slid from Azrael's face.

'Kira?'

'Did you leave any of those wine bottles intact?'

Azrael tilted his head like a confused baby bird. 'Yes. There are hundreds contained in that room.'

'Good. Let's stay down here a bit longer. I need that bottle of shiraz you were going for.'

# Blake - 44

Blake slept. But exhaustion did not make for simple, or pleasant, slumber. A tree haunted these dreams. Not the one she lay bound to. Another far worse. It was an unimpressive specimen, for all the horror it had delivered. A gnarled trunk, bark peeling away from its upper reaches. A bland shade of dull brown mixed with lighter greys. Branches mostly bare, creating a skeletal effect.

She stood at the base of the skeleton. The glare of lights came from behind and she turned. Headlights. In her dream Blake opened her mouth. Screamed. Not a sound left her. She tried to lift her arms, wave at the vehicle to turn away. But where her limbs should have been, there was metal. Dull metal, not catching the blaze of the oncoming catastrophe. The weight of her own body sucked her down, the soil crumbling beneath her feet. Dirt melting into rank pools of mud. Still, she tried to wave back the approaching car, tried to scream at the driver to focus on the road. Get back on the road. But still the light kept coming, growing larger and larger. Twin comets rushing headlong.

Sound did not have a place in this world. Utter silence wrapped around each and every terrible thing. In Blake's right hand a cell phone appeared, and on its tiny screen a single name shone in emerald green.

Kira.

Beneath, a symbol of a telephone receiver. A call being made.

Blake screamed into her void, tried to fling the phone away, but it had melted into the metal, and her hand and device were one. The mud sucked her down, diminishing her. Removing the only obstacle in the way of the car. The comet was on her now, blazing over her. Unhindered. And as it ploughed into the skeleton, every bone in Blake's body shattered in unison.

*You are death.*

Cruel words, made all the worse for the voice that carried them. Her father's familiar rumble, and his laughter echoing around her.

Her eyes flew open, and Blake sucked in air, desperate to fill her lungs. She gritted her teeth against the pain filling her body.

Every inch of her shook. The splinter at her wrist hot as an ember pressed to her skin. Overhead, the great wolf's head tilted to one side, a baleful eye regarding her. The glass at the iris was illuminated as though someone held a light behind it.

*You. If not for you.*

Blake groaned and her voice echoed in the confines of the shrine. Her crumbling mind leaked vitriol. If not for you. If not for making that call. Cancelling that dinner with Kira and her father. She closed her eyes, but even that caused discomfort. Open again. And the wolf had one paw raised as if to strike, alongside the Syranian beast's tail curved over its powerful body, a scorpion about to run her through. Carvings could not move. Could not end this.

That was a shame.

*Am . . . me . . . here. Blake.*

At least her father had retreated from the whispers. This voice not remotely like his. Not like any whisper she'd heard before. This one wasn't soaked with acid.

*Blake.*

In fact, it was no whisper at all, but rather a shout coming from a great distance.

Hands grasped her shoulders and pulled her upwards. Blake took aim and found her arms not so leaden as in the dream, but even still, the swing would not have hurt the proverbial fly. She had nothing left to give.

'Blake, it is Cym. Stay calm.'

The weight of the cuff around her neck disappeared, and her head dropped back, her neck no longer capable of holding it upright, and she found a soft pillow to meet her. Cym cradled her shoulders against his arm, shifting so that her head rested against his chest.

'What are you doing?' The words dribbled from her, spit mixing with blood.

*The betrayer. It would please you to see him burn.*

This was a more familiar whisper. Hissing and bubbling right up close. Each word a nail driven into her skull.

'Circumstances have changed, and they are in your favour. I have advised the captain and the Messenger that, under these altered conditions, it would be extremely unwise for me to be the only one capable of repairing the carapaces. They agreed, but I fear they hold you for a greater ransom.'

His words drifted around her, not sinking down to meet her completely. Her shadow watched her, still standing outside the shrine but far more defined than she'd known before.

'I cannot remove all of your suffering, Blake,' Cym was saying. 'The goddess will not allow it, but it will be lessened.'

*Hate. Hate him.*

The Syranian lifted her, and Blake's scream echoed around the confines. As the sound faded, a voice reached her.

*Blake. I'm here . . .*

Not Cym. Her head rested against his chest; any words he uttered would have caught against her ear. Nor was it the venomous whispers. She was splintering into pieces. Groaning, Blake knocked her head against Cym's chest.

'Stay still, Blake.' Cym spoke softly. His breath was like flame against her skin. 'Hold on. Your burden will ease as soon as we leave the Orientation Room.'

Leaving? Wasn't she supposed to die here? He took a step and her bones cracked. This time her scream came from a distance, muffled. Bright spots danced in her vision. Cym moved quickly, striding out of the shrine. Each of the three steps down to the Orientation Room floor created more fractures. Blake's screams rang hoarse; even her vocal cords were crumbling.

From beyond the chaos, Cym spoke to her. 'Listen to me, Blake. Kira is very much alive. Azrael protects her, they are still free. Do you hear me?'

Blake did not acknowledge him, the agony of speaking too overwhelming for her. But his words parted the clouded stupor she found herself in. Kira was alive. And free.

Cym strode towards the doors that would lead her out of her prison. And in that bright crystalline moment, the shadow stranger was a stranger no more. A very familiar silhouette stood just left of the opening doors. Nothing blurry about him now. There was no doubting who it was. He was the only friend Kira had ever introduced her to. But more than that, his features had been burned into Blake's mind the night she'd watched him die. Over and over. On the video playback from the Wheel and Barrow.

If Cym noticed the only other person in the room, he made no sign of it, carrying Blake straight past Perry.

## Tamas - 45

Tamas nursed his cast-bound hand against his chest and edged back the heavy curtains, elaborate crushed-gold satin he didn't recall approving when the renovations on the penthouse had been underway, with his free hand. They seemed an unnecessary opulence, but then again, the build in New Weston had taken place some time ago. He may well have been seeking a distraction from the endless waiting, while Blake and Cym and their team had worked on the carapaces. The goddess's visits had been intermittent in the early days. At one point he did not receive a Calling in almost a year.

And the old fears had crept in, keeping him awake at night. Making him wonder if his moment had come and gone, if Tamas was bound to suffer the same plight as his mother and his grandfather. The blood of a demigod had run in their veins, but they'd died unfulfilled, never truly having served the goddess and brought Her instructions to the mortals, creating Her masterpiece. It would be like Mozart being denied a piano, or Rembrandt a paintbrush. And it must have been utter agony.

Now, Tamas smiled down at the New Weston cityscape, the utukku shifting within him. A gift. The goddess's own words.

*Take these utukku I gift to you.*

She'd bestowed honour on him. Entrusted Tamas. Used his body – that body his own mother had so readily declared pathetic and incapable – to impart Her will. Indeed, he was thoroughly used. Bruises still held a dull ache, and the skin beneath the coral-style cast itched to be scratched. He shifted his shoulders, nerves sharp edged with the utukku's restlessness. There was a minute part of him that wished she were not dead, his mother. So that she could witness what he had become. His skin seemed barely able to contain the flesh and bone beneath it. He had never felt so . . . large . . . formidable. Undeniable.

And yet, he had failed his goddess in the task set to him. Enkidu had been desperately close when they'd raided the farmhouse, and he'd escaped. Eluding Ereshkigal's gift.

Tamas stared down at the bright lights of New Weston radiating like a thousand miniature suns beneath him. A massive city. Home to millions of humans.

Two years. Twenty-four months, since he'd left the Facility for any reasonable amount of time. Now, here he was. In a city of millions. Barely any sweat upon his brow. His breathing steady. Tamas watched office workers in one of the nearby buildings. Considering it was almost midnight, their numbers were few. What a tedious existence. Their heads in their screens, typing inane emails, organising dull meetings, while somewhere beneath them, in that sprinkling of light, extraterrestrial beings guided creatures of the underworld through the streets, on the hunt for a demigod.

Now *that* was pathetic.

'Your tea, sir.'

Startled, Tamas jerked on the curtain—and instantly admonished himself. That insipid, trembling wreck he'd been, even as recently as a few weeks ago, had to be dead and buried. He'd hidden behind an AI mask when he'd travelled with Reuben – searching for the Lesser and Enkidu and finding the witches in their little farmhouse atop the hill. Perhaps if he had not cowered behind the tech – and acted like the Messenger of the gods that he was – Enkidu would not have slipped his grasp. Tamas turned and made eye contact with the heavily made-up woman awaiting him. Tamas held her gaze.

'Thank you, Clara.' The barest tremble moved through his fingers, but it was the utukku that moved him. Not awkwardness. Scents of ginger and lemon wafted from the bright red mug she handed him. And there was no mistaking the shake in her hands. Rings formed in the liquid. It seemed impossible, but there it was. Tamas unnerved her.

'My pleasure, sir,' Clara said, smile too wide, houndstooth skirt too form-fitting, and her eagerness irksome. 'Reuben is expected in about fifteen minutes and—'

'Yes, I'm aware.' About Reuben, at least. Tamas took a sip of the tea; it was searingly hot, but the discomfort distracted him from the ever-growing movement of the utukku. He didn't need this woman, with her blood lips and heavy eyeliner, to tell him Reuben's helicopter approached. The utukku sensed the nearness of their kind, and their crawl beneath his skin grew feverish.

'Very well, I will—' She spun to face the door, hips moving like water. 'Ah, the detainee is here as you requested. Where would you like them to place her?'

Three guards escorted the white-haired woman found at the farmhouse; the only survivor of that disastrous mission. While Tamas had wasted time with the witches atop their hill, just five kilometres away Enkidu had been destroying the Arc Team. For reasons he did not yet fathom, the utukku had failed to trace him. And Tamas needed to know why. Needed to understand. He gave himself a self-congratulatory nod for deciding against having her brought to the Facility. If the supermundanes of the world were being stirred up, it didn't seem prudent to take one of them into the heart of the Facility, right where the Tier Waters generated their power. And this woman, despite appearances, held power.

'Somewhere there.' He made a vague gesture towards the wide champagne-coloured couch on the far side of the room. And it took only one look at the bedraggled, shackled woman they hauled into the room to know he would be undertaking his questioning alone. She didn't have the energy to place one foot in front of the other, let alone attempt to bolt to freedom in the heavily fortified penthouse. 'Then leave us. Have Reuben join us when he arrives.'

The bodyguard had returned from a fruitless hunt through the valleys and farmlands around ground zero; the lonely road where Enkidu had destroyed both Facility property and human personnel alike. With Kira at his side. Even now, recalling the footage delivered by Captain Nex, Tamas could not help but clench his uninjured fist, incredulity and anger bubbling in unison.

The woman was dragged into the room, quite literally. Her legs remained limp, her toes scraping the ground. She'd been held less than forty-eight hours, yet her appearance suggested a lifetime as a convict. She was still clad in the lime-green velour tracksuit she'd been apprehended in, and her stark-white hair was an eruption of white atop her head. A couple of childish, colourful clips still clung to strands here and there. Lines roadmapped her face. Her lips were a sickly bluish white, but her skin was an utterly unnatural shade of orange. Dirt marked her clothing, remnants of the windstorm she and her friends had churned up against Reuben and the Facility entourage. She might be dragging her feet, but Tamas could not let himself forget the strength she'd shown against them earlier. And indeed, now. The Syranian serum had been injected into her veins, and all they'd gotten was gibberish. Talk of some deity she worshipped called the Maiden. A goddess, she declared, who was going to be 'very pissed off about all this'. She also muttered about her love for a veil, and the hope that someone called Bradley would bite off everyone's testicles.

Pure vitriol spewed at him through her gaze. She thrust her hands – bound almost to the tips of her fingers in a restrictive mesh – towards the guard trying to push her down onto the couch.

'I don't want to sit on the damn couch!' she hollered. 'Get lost.'

The guard raised his arm, readying to take a swing. Not the first, if the bruises on her cheeks were anything to go by.

'Leave her,' Tamas said. 'Go.'

Clara moved to follow orders immediately, but Tamas caught the rise of eyebrows from one of the guards, a woman he recognised from the lower levels of the Facility but whose name escaped him. Or indeed, he'd never known. The foursome filed from the room, and he was alone with the white witch.

Gibberish or not, she had without doubt been in Azrael's company and, along with the two men at the farmhouse, had resisted Reuben's arrival with considerable preternatural strength. At the same time, Azrael had been killing Facility soldiers and destroying multiple grimalkin. From the start, Ereshkigal had informed Tamas that Enkidu was unaware of his true self. Certainly, that had been so in the Facility in the days after his arrival, when he'd been no more than a zombie the Syranians could train on. But there was no trace of the mindless being in the footage taken by the grimalkin. And Enkidu had uttered the goddess's name.

Enkidu was self-aware. Something even Captain Nex had declared, though the Syranian could not know the full gravity of the declaration, still believing Enkidu . . . Azrael . . . to be a gallu of little consequence.

Now there was a further development ¬– the flying beast encountered by Agar and Eron earlier that day. An uneasy sense of loss of control gripped Tamas. And it did not sit well. When the news had come in, Tamas had decided once and for all that it was time to leave the Facility and seek out some answers.

The utukku were as keen as he was to extract them from their guest, and the pinpricks of their movement inflamed his skin. He pressed at his ears where the ringing held at its incessant pitch. It would have been nice if there could be just one moment of being the Messenger that wasn't uncomfortable.

'Don't be looking at me like that. You're wasting your time with me,' the witch spat. Actually *spat*. The globule disappeared into the shaggy lengths of the black rug at her feet. 'I don't know where they are, and even if I did, I'd tell you nothing. They've already pricked me full of whatever bullshit was in that needle, and if they were hoping for the truth, they got it. You are a bunch of bastards. Killing innocent people. Messing where you don't belong –' Her head jerked to one side, a birdlike move, and her gaze ran up and down Tamas's body. 'Well, well. Don't you reek. I see you are touched. Can barely stand the stench of you. So now I'm finally meeting some of the brains behind the brawn, huh? You that Tamas guy she's been –' Her mouth snapped closed, and there was blissful silence.

The Syranian serum had extracted little from her but an encyclopedia of foul curses. Kira must have loved this woman's company. Tamas folded his arms across his belly. How that messed-up slut had become central to all this was one thing he could not comprehend.

'I am Tamas, yes. And I'm sure that Kira spoke highly of me.' Tamas took a sip of tea, using the cup to hide his grimace. The utukku were making it hard to catch his breath. 'I don't have any serum. I employ another method to encourage communication. You saw an example of it when we visited you at your quaint little farm.'

'Fuck you.' Another globule sailed onto the shag pile. The woman was truly Kira's equal in refinement. But the way she stared at him—no, stared *into* him—made him wary.

'No, thank you.' Tamas focused on the liquid in his teacup, the vapours warm against his skin. He should get on with it, use the utukku, ensure he knew all he could, and then dispose of her. But he was enjoying the way his words fell so smoothly. Not even close to faltering. Certainly, the white witch's arrowing gaze made him uneasy, but that disquiet went both ways. The way she rocked back, just a little, every time he made direct eye contact, was exhilarating. He took another sip. Blake would look at him that way, too, before all was said and done. 'What is your name?'

'Leona Louise Kerr. Born in nineteen sixty-four, in London, England, to Jack Kerr—'

'Enough!' Tamas set down his teacup. The serum had some effect at least. He recognised the strain of the veins in her neck as she fought her own traitorous—and grating—vocal cords. Blake had done the same thing, but unlike the white witch, she had failed to keep her details down to the very basics. 'Leona, what do you see when you look at me?'

He approached her, taking his time, enjoying the way she tried to shuffle back onto the cushion.

'Ms Kerr to the likes of you, thanks very much.' She shook her head, her array of hair clips bobbing madly. The woman was ridiculous. 'Though you might be drenched in brightness, you are no god, I see that much. Don't get yourself confused, boy –'

'What do you see?' The utukku rose, lifting with the hum of a thousand bees and threading their way through him headed for his hands.

Leona Louise Kerr leaned forward and met his gaze. 'Fractures. You walk with the bright ones, but you are dull at your core. A servant at best. You are no different to me. And my mistress has a message for yours – get off our bloody planet. Your time here is done.'

Despite the building pain of the utukku's dance in his blood, Tamas smiled and bent down, his face only a few centimetres from hers. 'At least I am a servant capable of doing something useful. And my mistress is very far from done. If the best yours can do is that oversized flying bird, She might want to be careful whom She threatens.'

He raised his hands and grasped her head between them. Leona screeched. There was no other word for it. Parrots being put through a meat grinder would make a less offensive sound. But he held fast and let the utukku find their way into her cells, those sand-grain shards burrowing fast and furious into her body. She took a while to bleed, and it didn't run quite as violently as Reuben's had, perhaps because the utukku were a fraction of what he had used on Reuben. The guard still carried the bulk of the goddess's gift with him as he continued the search. Leona's screeching stopped abruptly, and a gurgle erupted from her throat. Rose-coloured dribble ran from her lips. Tamas moved back, stepping wide to ensure none of her saliva found his sneakers. He scanned the room, seeking something to wipe his bloodied hands on. None of the white witch's blood would be meeting his clothing, that much was certain.

She slumped till her forehead looked in danger of meeting her lap. Frowning, Tamas halted his search. The woman was muttering under her breath.

'What did you say?'

She jerked her head up, one of her clips flying free. The whites of her eyes showed. 'I said, go back to hell.'

Leona Louise Kerr might not have appeared athletic, or even remotely fit, but looks, in her case, were very much deceptive. She launched herself off the couch and darted around the low lacquered coffee table.

'Where do you think you're running to?' Tamas said.

She might escape from this room, at the very most, but any intention of leaving the penthouse was laughable.

But she did not head for the door. Instead, she raced to where he'd set down his teacup on an ornamental serving cart alongside a black leather armchair. Leona's muttering pitched higher, all uttered in a language he could not pinpoint. She lifted the cup from its saucer and flicked it so that the remaining liquid—at least half a cup— sprayed into the air. Now it would be prudent to call for assistance, but Tamas remained silent, curious to see just exactly what the woman thought she could achieve with the utukku in her system and his guards thick around the penthouse. Let her show him what this Maiden of hers could do.

The water rose high above Leona's head, the droplets catching every bit of light in the room and twinkling diamond-like as they moved. Those liquid diamonds should have begun to fall, gravity's effect dragging them down towards the woman and dousing her. But that did not happen. The droplets hung above her, as though caught on invisible strings. The few remaining utukku that still swam within him pushed towards the surface of his skin, and the tips of his bloodied fingers tingled the same way they had when he'd pulled the utukku from Blake back into his own body.

This little stunt was no longer bemusing. Tamas took a step towards Leona, and as his foot hit the thickness of the shaggy rug, the droplets showered down on her. Splitting or multiplying, Tamas wasn't sure, but there was no doubt that there were far more now than had left the cup. The white witch tilted her head, letting the droplets spatter against her face. Blood ran with the fluid, soft pink against the blatant pumpkin shade of her skin. Tamas winced, the sensation in his hands drifting from uncomfortable to downright painful. And all at once the space between where he stood and where Leona bled filled with the tiny particles of the utukku.

'No . . .' But there was no denying it. Somehow, she had banished the goddess's gift from her body. Tamas gritted his teeth.

The utukku swarmed against his hands, rushing back into the microscopic tears in his skin, flooding his system.

Leona dropped to her knees, a dazed expression on her face, blood staining the lime-green tracksuit. 'Oh boy. That wasn't pleasant.'

Fighting to keep his composure, Tamas glared at her. He didn't want her to have any inkling that what she'd just done shocked him. Showing such a weakness seemed ill-advised. But what in all the holy realms of Kur had just happened?

Any answer would have to wait. Reuben staggered into the room, his clothes blood soaked. Red ran from every part of his face, thick and dark beneath his nostrils, streams down the side of his neck where blood forced itself from his ears.

'Reuben . . .' Tamas heard the desperation in that single uttered word – so much for hiding his weakness – but it was a truly horrific sight.

'Help me . . .' Rueben didn't speak so much as gurgle.

Two guards rushed in behind him, Clara close behind, clutching a bundle of towels. 'Sir, apparently he started to deteriorate on descent. He won't listen to anyone else; he was determined to get to you.'

She flung one of the towels around Reuben's shoulders, as if that might somehow stop the torrent of blood escaping him. Tamas ran towards his bodyguard but didn't reach him before Reuben collapsed.

'Tamas—'

He began to convulse, torso rigid and arms jerking so hard Tamas had to dodge to miss being struck in the face. He grabbed Reuben's right wrist, just above the inhibitor bracelet, and pressed his body weight down against it. One of the other guards did the same on the other arm while Clara knelt at his feet.

'We need to get him to the hospital ,' she cried.

'Sweet Maiden's laces, has he had those damn things inside him since you attacked us at the farmhouse?' Leona stood over them, wiping at her face with her bound hands. 'He's human, you fool. It's too much.'

'Get back, witch,' Tamas hissed. He tried to keep hold of Reuben, desperately trying to get the utukku to withdraw. But Reuben's blood and violent movement made a sure grip nearly impossible. And the utukku had become deaf to him. Those already within Tamas darted like wasps in his gut, but his fingers didn't tingle and his blood didn't heat, which had both, until now, been sure signs that the utukku outside his body were returning. The entities were refusing to do Tamas's bidding. And tearing Reuben apart.

'He's going to die—' Leona said.

'I said get back!' Tamas screamed. Death was obvious. It was staining the whole world red. Tamas's breath came in short, sharp bursts, and panic made his heart into a manic machine.

Reuben was dying, right in front of him. Tamas was about to be robbed of the sole human being who had not abandoned him.

'For goodness sake, ' Leona dropped to her knees alongside him, 'get your devils under control, boy. You are the master, and if you don't start acting like one, this man here will die. And I've had just about enough of death for the time being. Keep your focus.'

'Get away from me.' Tamas dug his fingernails into Reuben's skin and pressed the side of his hand against the inhibitor bracelet, the tightness of the metal finally enabling him to find some purchase. A faint sensation prickled in his fingertips.

'Calm yourself, lad. I'm going to help you,' Leona said. 'Though the Maiden only knows why.'

She laid her hands alongside his own on Reuben's arm. And immediately the tingle in his fingers turned into a roar, as though he'd slammed his hand onto a hotplate. Tamas cried out but refused to let go. Heat tore through his body, and so did the utukku. Torrents of them, streaming out of Reuben's body and back into his own. Their pace was breathtaking. No papercuts this time; their frenzy turned them into knives, driving hard against Tamas's skin, forcing their way back into the darkness inside of him. It was sheer brilliant agony. Alongside him, Leona let out a high-pitched squeal, but she, too, did not let go. The violent shudders and jerks of Reuben's body subsided. His head thrashed side to side, but his torso did not lift as though trying to snap him in half. Tamas bowed his head, jaw clenched so hard there would be broken teeth after this for sure. But it was working. The utukku – his devils – were returning to his control.

People were shouting. At Tamas, over him, and all around him.

'Shoot her, shoot her!' Clara screamed.

Tamas lifted his head and bared his teeth. 'Don't touch her.' He shifted his body so that it blocked Leona from the gun being levelled at her head. 'I said do not touch her.' His command filled the room, booming with an echo that threatened to shatter windows. The pitch of it lifted the unfortunate guard wielding the weapon and hurled him across the room.

It was over a moment later. Tamas sat back on his heels, his blood-drenched hands limp at his sides. The utukku buried and silent.

Leona's shoulders heaved with each breath, her snow-white hair damp at her forehead. Her hands still rested on Reuben's. 'Well, that was . . .'

Whatever it was, Tamas didn't learn. Leona leaned hard to one side, eyes rolling back in her head. And in a slow and steady movement, she toppled to the ground.

'Sir? Sir?' An urgent voice shook Tamas from his stupor. 'Permission to attend, sir.'

Tamas blinked up at the solemn face. A woman probably the same age as Leona stood over him with a kit in one hand. It took another few seconds for his muddled head to compute. A medic. She wanted to check on Reuben.

'Why are you asking me, you idiot?' Tamas shifted onto his knees, his jeans soaked through with blood. 'Fix him. Don't let him die.' He hesitated and stabbed a crimson fingertip towards Leona. 'Her either. She does not die.'

## Kira - 46

Kira surveyed the bath and its rising water level. Timing was critical. One screw up, and things got ugly. Run the cold water a little too strong, and you had a tub of lukewarm disappointment. But run the hot water at full bore for too long, and things didn't end well. Yeah, sure, you could get in, slowly. Give your body time to adjust to the roasting. The hotter the better, so far as Kira was concerned. But death by slow boil snuck up on you. Wasn't until you were the colour of beetroot and you couldn't feel your toes that you realised the water had been too damn hot. The number of times she'd had to lie naked on her bed for thirty minutes to recover was not something she was proud about.

But this time? A dip of her toes, a sweep of flesh fingers through the water, and Kira smiled.

'Fucking perfect.'

She turned off the faucets and hooked her fingers into her black satin pants, the ones with wine stains around the ankles. Nina knew her shit when it came to clothes and wine choices, Kira would give her that much. That bottle Kira'd opened after the shit storm with Azrael was probably the nicest thing to ever slide across her tongue. But Az hadn't been so sure. He might have been into the champagne back at the casino, but he wasn't so keen on the red. No appreciation for tannins. Kira felt it was her solemn duty not to let the opened bottle go to waste, so while she cleaned up the mess, she cleaned up the bottle. Had she told him about the phone call to Eron? It was all a little hazy. Az hadn't followed her when she'd come back upstairs after an hour or so. She got that. Sometimes a guy, or a demigod, or a wild man, whatever he was, just needed some time out. Kira had watched terrible reality TV with the miniature wizard, and now it was after midnight and Vail was sleeping, still burritoed in blankets on the couch. He'd told her Rossiter had taken a leak at some point, so the big man was alive, which was good. But he was snoring show tunes now; Kira could hear him from the bathroom. And as for Nina, no idea where she was. Which was fine. It had given Kira's ovaries time to chill the fuck out.

Her pants slid to the floor, followed close behind by her panties . The entire external wall of this bathroom was glass. What wasn't in this place? But the to-die-for views were gone. Night-time had shat everywhere with blacker-than-black inkiness.

Kira pulled off her shirt and then stepped into the tub without glancing in the mirror. The wine was humming nicely, subtle. No danger of a hangover. No point ruining it by staring at the weird-ass metal clawing its way to freedom on her shoulder. She was getting used to it anyway. Sure. Yeah. No biggie. Nothing to see here.

'Oh man, this is going to be so—'

A cry filtered down the hallway. Pitchy, strained, and containing just one word. 'Kira!'

'He's kidding me, right?' Kira asked the bath bomb fizzing itself stupid in the tub.

The cry came again, with a dollop more panic on top. 'Kira, where are you?'

If Vail was just having a nightmare, she was going to drown him in her perfectly temperate bath. Kira hopped out of the water, feet slapping against the heated sandstone tiles. Shirt back on, silk pants on. Forget underwear, this was going to be a quick trip. Sort out the kid. Sing him back to sleep. Then soak time.

Kira jogged the hallway, past Rossiter's room, past the door that had taken her down to the garage. She reached the archway leading into the lounge room, and her breath caught in her throat.

There are certain things that a girl expects to see in a lounge room: couch, a television, maybe a couple of shaggy throw pillows. Not this. A bird. Some oversized black parrot using Vail's blanket-laden shoulder as a makeshift perch. Dark as pitch with red around the eyes. One of its wings didn't look so good.

'Vail . . . you okay?' Kira said.

A door opened in the hall behind her. Then came the thud of heavy feet on the floorboards.

'Kira? What the hell is going on?' Rossiter walked towards her, one hand at his balls, the other scratching his face. The paisley boxer shorts he wore were about two sizes too small. It was quite the sight, and she'd give him plenty of shit later. Now wasn't the time. Kira raised a finger to her lips.

'Stay back,' she hissed.

'Kira, what do I do?' Vail sounded as old as his baby face looked. Like, ten.

Holy crap, Kira wasn't exactly the bird whisperer. How did she know? Moving slowly, arms raised, she edged closer to where Vail sat still as a green-tinged statue.

'Shoo, fuck off.' She waved her hands as if she were cooling a cake. Must have looked ridiculous, and the bird didn't give a shit. 'Get off him, go on. Piss off.'

Closer now, lots more waving. The thing's head jerked back, and it tilted the other red-rimmed eye towards her. The look clearly said, *Bitch what is your problem?* She knelt on the edge of the couch. If she wanted to, Kira could lean in and punch it off Vail's shoulder, she was that close now. A black eyeball darted back and forth, and the bird's head rocked from side to side. Was it checking her out? Planning on how it was going to tear her own eyes from their sockets? Fuck, birds were freaky.

Vail gasped. 'Oh, whoa. Kira . . . ouch . . . don't come closer. It doesn't like it.'

'What's it doing?'

'Digging its claws in,' Vail squeaked through clenched teeth.

Rossiter chose that moment to get involved. 'I'll deal with this.'

The human hairless sasquatch stomped around the couch, giant hands reaching for the bird. In fairness to the avian, Kira probably would have gone bat-shit crazy, too, if that pillar of humanity had gone for her. The squawk it let out was monumental, guaranteed to tear paint off walls. Wings expanded, smacking Vail in the face, throwing the blanket hood from his head. The kid's cry joined the bird's. And she glimpsed something dark on Vail's shoulder. A stain. Blood?

'Vail.' Kira wasn't entirely sure what she intended to do. All she knew was the kid was getting hurt, and it pissed her off. Big time. She lunged forward, reaching for the bird. At the same time, Blackie the crazed parrot, mirrored her. They met in a clash of feathers and curses. The impact threw Kira backwards off the couch. The armadillo took some of the brunt – its extended form covered her shoulder blade – but it didn't manage to stop the air from being knocked out of her. The bird perched on her chest, needle-point beak way too close to her face for comfort, and the claws Vail had bitched about digging into her tits.

The screeching was the stuff of nightmares. And deafness. If Kira wasn't winded, she'd be shouting, *Shut the fuck up!* Instead she let her hands do the talking and swung at the feathery lump sitting on her. The armadillo hit pay dirt, and an almighty squawk rang out, a sound that could slice open a person's brain. But the damn insane parrot wasn't dislodged by her blow. It clung to the armadillo for dear life. Fuck, the thing weighed a tonne. The bird, not the armadillo. Weren't birds' bones hollow? And why the fuck was that random fact coming to her right now as a feathered friend of Satan was trying to rip her metal arm from her body? Christ almighty, make it stop. Wings beat at her, admittedly not painful, but not her idea of a great night in, either. Through the calamity, someone called her name. Actually, a whole bunch of someones did. Vail's higher pitch rang clear against Rossiter's bellow. Then a new voice joined the fray.

'Kira, remain calm.'

'You fucking remain calm, Az. Get this thing off me.'

He knelt down beside her in a honey-wrapped package of sublime prettiness, reaching for her. Az's fingers touched her metal wrist.

Everything blurred, grew cloudy as though she'd spent too long in a chlorine pool.

Kira blinked like a madwoman, but it just made it worse. Might as well have been buried in a snowbank. And what was with the silence? Heavy and impenetrable. Jesus, was she dead? Because if she was, then this deal sucked ass. Dead was supposed to mean shirking off the old mortal coil and all that. Getting rid of all the shit that came with being human. The memories, the mistakes. But all that crap was still there, rolling around in her head. The crash. The funeral. The loneliness. Fresh as a daisy.

The snowy wonderland peeled away, layer after layer vanishing, and the world beyond it started to shift into focus. Maybe this was concussion, a weird dream state or something. Had to be. Because she was flying. Soaring over a landscape that was rushing up to meet her. There was no sense of falling or of the air moving against her. No sensation at all.

Her free fall closed in on a figure moving through the foggy world below. She drew closer, and the figure drew into crystal-clear definition.

Eron.

She was staring at Eron. Every long centimetre of him. Damn. The boy was good enough to eat. That neck, long and lean, leading the eye to trace up over his pillow lips and then along a nose a god had built. Hell if it didn't hollow out her belly to see him. At least, Kira thought it did. Her belly didn't seem quite with her, as if it were still up in the clouds she was pretty sure she was in. But it was hard to give two fucks when Eron was right there. A few metres away. Lifting one shoulder, just a fraction higher than the other, like he always did when he was concentrating hard. Kira soared past him, and the part of her sitting way up high in the clouds freaked out.

No, no, no. Don't leave. Shit, fuck. She wasn't ready.

Her point of view arced left, gliding in a wide circle. High above Eron. And in a sure sign that her life was now certifiable, her situation made sudden sense. She wasn't flying. That psycho parrot was. Kira would bet her onyx credit card limit that she was— 'cause this is how she rolled now—a goddamn bird. Inside its teeny brain, looking out its goggly eyes, but hearing nothing with its ears. Did birds have ears? Anyway, point was, it was tomb-at-the-bottom-of-the-ocean quiet.

Fine. If it meant she got to undress Eron with her eyes for a second or two, Kira was going to own this avian thing like a motherfucker.

Eron wasn't at the Facility. That much was clear. He stood in an alleyway, fully clothed. Dressed in his standard garb, the all-black pants and long-sleeved shirt, which set off his moonlight-pale skin like a charm. He stood alongside a snow-white Land Rover. Nice and understated. And looking very out of place in the alley filled with stock standard alleyway stuff: industrial bins, junk in piles, drains that never seemed to run dry. Kira's bird vision went stationary as she perched on the gutter of a low-set building overlooking the alley. Eron slipped a cap over his white hair, tucking up the long strands beneath it. A door on the Rover opened, and a second guy stepped out. Definitely not one of the aliens. Even the stockiest of the Syranians, Gren, couldn't hold a candle to this dude. Rossiter would give him a run for his money, but based on the way this guy moved, heavy arms lifted from his sides as if he were already coiled to take a swing, Kira wouldn't place any bets on the big man taking him out.

She'd met pit bulls like this before. Found them on the doors at seedy nightclubs, permanent sneers attached to their lips. Miserable fucks. Life had put their balls in a vice, and they liked to share the pain. Eron and his thug moved out of the alleyway and onto a main street that teemed with people. Lots and lots of humans lining up alongside the road, some with chairs. Settling in. A parade or something maybe?

Okay. Well, on the oddness scale this was up there. She and Eron had had their asses handed to them when they'd gotten busted sneaking out of the Facility. The aliens were on a strict you-ain't-going-nowhere curfew. So what the hell was Eron doing here, strolling down a main street packed with people?

Her bird self lifted off the rooftop and moved higher, giving her an eagle-eyed – or rather, parrot-eyed – view of the city. One building in particular caught her attention. A white dome-shaped structure to the right.

Presley Stadium.

They were in New Weston. Kira had watched enough
boring-ass cricket matches with ball-hitting fanatic Perry to know
that much. She was usually hungover as all hell in Perry's bed,
sucking back a hair-of-the-dog beer and a spliff, while he went on
and fucking on about how awesome Presley Stadium was, how the
groundskeepers did an amazeballs job, blah blah. It was grass. Who
gave a shit?

Parrot-vision moved down and skimmed over the top of
the crowd, moving in closer to Eron and the ball buster, who was a
few strides ahead shoving his way through the sea of people lined
up along the road. There were a hell of a lot of colours in this
crowd, bright and fantastic, mixed with good old beige, shocking
pink wigs worn by people with made-up faces, walking alongside
Mr and Mrs Jones and their two point five kids. Some people
jumped and gyrated. Dancing, she presumed, or having a group
seizure. Some kind of Mardi Gras then.

From her birdy height, Kira had a top-notch view of people
throwing Eron second, third, and fourth glances. One cheeky son
of a bitch—poured into a pair of sparkling silver hot pants—made
a grab for Eron's ass. Kira couldn't see his face, birdbrain held back
a bit, but she could picture it perfectly. Eron's eyebrows arching but
causing no wrinkles on his forehead. Lips parting a fraction, wet
and pink, a soft gasp escaping him. Man, what she wouldn't do to

hear that again. Yeah. She knew the look exactly. She'd triggered it more than once.

The snowbank rushed up, dunking Kira back into the all-white world she'd first found herself in. Bird-vision was wiped clean, but not for long. The peel back was super quick this time, lifting like a curtain on a stage. When Kira blinked her way back into her feathered friend, Eron and his burly sidekick were somewhere new. A roadblock of some kind stood between the car they sat in and a street that looked like it had been hit by a bomb. Shop fronts were burned out, cafe chairs strewn around the streets. All at once the memory knocked her on the head. New Weston riots. She and Vail had seen it on the news earlier. Jesus. If she was still looking at New Weston, then this wasn't just a bunch of restless kids. The place was demolished. Blue and white ribbons cordoned off some of the more unstable shells of buildings along the road. Her bird's-eye view dipped and moved down nice and low, gliding to one of the industrial bins. So close to Eron that if Kira could get her maybe-wing to stretch, she could probably touch him. And shit that was a nice idea.

The image shivered, rattled around a little, then bam, they were back. And all hell was breaking loose. Eron right at the heart of it, arms raised with a burst of light coming from his hands – blasting the shit out of a bunch of cops, throwing them across the road, virtually into the ruined storefronts. Their bodies fell in heaps way too fucked up to be anything but bad. Really bad. Eron's cap had fallen from his head, and the sunlight caught his white hair, turning it a sunset orange. And his face. The face that could melt Kira's panties right off, was twisted and scrunched into a horror mask. Distorted by a butt-ugly grin, teeth bared as though he not only wanted to fuck those cops over, he also wanted to eat them alive.

Her pretty boy had never been so ugly.

Kira was done. She wanted out of Dodge.

Birdy vision went straight up, down, then up, down, then up. Jerky, as though the parrot were bogged in invisible mud. But at least she couldn't see Eron anymore. There was only sky.

And then, there wasn't even that.

# Kira - 47

The snowstorm cleared in a heartbeat. Kira's eyes flew open. She was back in Nina's house, lying on her side alongside . . . what the hell was that?

'Jesus.' She threw herself away from the *thing* taking up most of the rug, and her roll sent her crashing into Nina's knees.

'It's okay, Kira.' Vail's voice, coming from behind her, but Kira only had eyes for her own chest. A sticky, dark goo—blacker than the black of the satin shirt—plastered the material to her chest. 'What is this shit? Oh my god, did it slime me?' She lifted her shirt, intending to rip the damn thing off, but Nina placed a firm hand on her shoulder.

'Will everyone just calm down. Anzu's blood will not harm you, Kira—' The woman's hair looked as if she'd just left the salon, and her satin lavender shift cupped every curve, spaghetti straps straining against the titty load.

'I cannot be calm with a fucking deformed ostrich lying beside me.'

It wasn't the greatest comparison Kira had ever made. The thing had a head big as solid as a lion's, complete with a shaggy mane of rust-tipped black feathers, but a beak jutted out of the muzzle, steel grey and curved like a scythe.

She let her satin T-shirt settle back over her shoulders. 'What corner of hell did that crawl out of?'

This thing *was* as big as an ostrich, but its wings would have looked more at home on a giant eagle. The left was banged up, some thick black ooze seeping from the top joint where a huge hooked claw curved like a crescent moon. Its body was a mass of jet-black feathers, with legs kind of like a chicken's, except five times the size, scaly, smoke grey, and with three talons on each that could pierce a tank. And this fowl had more than a busted wing. A bunch of deep gashes trailed down the right leg. And a whole lot of ooze ran free from the wounds. Stomach heaving, Kira's eyes returned to the head. The circle of red feathers around the eyes caught her attention.

'Holy shit, is that . . .' Oh god, just say it. No idea was too insane anymore. 'Is that . . . tell me that's not the parrot.'

'It is the parrot.' Vail again.

She swung toward the voice. The kid wasn't alone. 'Rossiter!' Kira cried.

The big man was down, lying in the doorway, legs in the lounge, head in the hall. Vail had dumped his blanket fort and held Rossiter's head in his lap. Az crouched at Rossiter's feet, his back to Kira, giving her a perfect view of a freshly shredded T-shirt and the great gashes in his faux skin where the slice-and-dice wings jutted from. A cold chill washed over her. 'Oh, Az, is Rossiter . . .' She couldn't even look. 'Fuck –'

'He's not dead. Passed out when Anzu transformed,' Nina said, all singsongy and perky. 'Couldn't handle the sound of growing bone, poor love. No, no one is dead, Kira. Not yet anyway. In fact, I've never felt so alive.'

Nina got all up in Kira's face and danced about as she spoke. 'You saw them. I know you did. And you got very excited about one of them; the shivers ran all through the recall. You weren't afraid, though, not even close. I'm going to bet it was the pretty silver-haired specimen that was getting you all hot and bothered; you've always loved a beautiful ass. And that ass is walking around with a greater gallu from the very pits of Kur, all suited up in a human suit, just like our friend Azrael. So I'm also putting money on them both being from that home of yours you despise so much, the Facility. Do I win?'

Kira just stared at Nina. Her cheeks were a deeper desert tone
than the rest of her face. Whatever had just gone on had the
handmaiden as worked up as she declared Kira to be. Bouncing out
of her skin. The woman needed to put on a bra, like yesterday. All
that bouncing made it hard to concentrate. Besides, a little mamma-
bear protective instinct was growling. Eron might have looked like a
rabid zombie on autokill, but Kira wasn't about to spill all his beans
to Nina.

'Get out of my way.' Kira elbowed past Miss Too Much Coke,
and peered over Az's shoulders. She kept one eye closed, so she
was already halfway to total blackout if she spotted any guts
hanging out of the R-man.

'He's really okay, Kira. Not a scratch, probably a headache
though.' Vail smiled at her, and she opened her eye . 'How about
you? That was pretty intense.' He nodded at Az. 'I don't think
Azrael liked what he saw, either. We had another wing incident.'

Az really needed to get that shit under control before
someone lost a head. Kira shook her own, slowly. The ooze on the
shirt caused the material to cling to her body, and shivers ran up her
flesh arm. 'I don't even know what that was –' aside from Eron
acting like the goddamn Terminator and hanging out with a dude
who looked as if he ate small children for breakfast.

'It was a recall from Anzu's memory. Images he wished us to
view.' Nina knelt beside the downed bird-lion-freak-thing, but her
gaze ran the length of Kira's body. 'It's quite impressive, and a little

119

odd, that you were able to see them, Kira. Aren't you just my little bundle of hidden talents?'

Oh, Nina had no idea. 'Yeah, well Little Miss Sunshine here is getting a bit sick of having random weird shit happen to her.'

Nina laughed. No. She giggled. School-girl high. 'But the random weird stuff is exactly what makes life interesting, Kira. I'm not going to pretend I'm not very, very turned on right now. You have no idea how dull this place can be. And it's gone from utter boredom to calamitous chaos in the space of a week. Somehow, Ereshkigal has reopened a gateway to this insufferable world. First, we are graced with Enkidu, thought long dead, and now her greatest servant walks the Earth. Divine games are afoot, and it is glorious.'

She bundled up one of Vail's discarded blankets and used it as a makeshift compress against the thing – Anzu's – wounded leg. From the waist up, Nina was the only one who didn't look as if she'd just been hit by a truck, but her knees were black with whatever the shit was that was seeping from the mangled parrot-thing, and the hem of her shift was poo-brown with stains.

'I am seeing more and more light at the end of a very dark tunnel, my friends. So much light. I don't think I've seen Anzu for close to a thousand years. I chose immortality in this world, but this poor bastard had it forced on him. A lesson to be learned there. Never steal from your god-master, or if you do, don't get caught. Case in point.' She pointed a black-gunk-coated finger at Anzu. 'But

I haven't come across him for so long that I thought he'd found a way out of this place – and was rather pissed he hadn't bothered to tell me his secret to ending immortality.'

The bird-thing let out a garbled groan, followed by a series of dull clicks.

Nina nodded. 'Yes, well, we may have an out now, my friend. If the goddess has found her way back into this world, that means there is a way *out* for us. And we can send everlasting life back to the hell it came from.' She clapped her goo-ridden hands.

Azrael rose to his feet, taking it slow. 'If you had spent time in the company of Agar, you would not be quite so flippant. The Four are base and cruel, Agar most of all. He showed me no mercy when he dragged me to Kur at the behest of Ereshkigal. I would gladly tear him limb from limb into a thousand living pieces, and feed each morsel to the Aqrabuamelu.'

Kira cringed. Partly because Az was being totally gross, partly because she'd experienced a fraction of the pain he'd gone through, and if she were him, she'd be feeding this guy to the fishes, too. But the cringe also meant – what the hell was with the crazy-ass names? Why couldn't they just have Sams or Bobs in this Kur place? An Aqrabuamelu? Sounded like a cocktail you could never order because you could never pronounce it.

Pinching the bridge of her nose, Kira focused back on the room. 'Who is Agar? That guy with Eron?' The huge one with a face like a smacked ass? Azrael knew what Eron looked like, so if they'd been feather-gazing at the same memories, chances were he was referring to Ass-face.

She gave herself a silent high five for just rolling with the fact that they had all just shared the same vision, dream, whatever, with the goop-covered dino-bird on the lounge room floor.

'Eron, hmm?' Nina purred. 'The pretty silver-haired one?'

'Yes,' Kira snapped. 'The one with the great ass.'

'The one you've bedded. On more than one occasion I suspect.'

Heat rose to Kira's cheeks. Christ almighty, since when did she blush about whom she'd screwed? Short answer, never.

'Can we focus on the important shit? Who I've banged really doesn't seem important right now.'

Nina tilted her head, a coy smile playing at her lips. 'No. Perhaps not. But whom you love could be of the utmost importance, in time. Who knows? Fate works in mysterious ways, as they say. And these are indeed mysterious times.'

Kira turned her back on Nina's smug, and achingly beautiful, face and repeated her question. 'Az, who is that guy? Is he like you?'

A greater gallu from the very pits of Kur, that's what Nina Stick My Nose In Your Personal Life had said earlier. And only bad things festered in pits.

Az paced over to the window, taking a wide berth around the panting Anzu. Someone really needed to get bird-thing a Band-Aid.

'That face is one created by the Facility, as was mine. But we could see what lay beneath.'

She scratched at the back of her neck, trying to reach an itch beneath the metal. 'The brightness', that's what Leona called it. And that's what Az could see. The stuff these supernaturals had in bucket loads, marking them out. The stuff Kira couldn't see. And she wasn't sure if that pissed her off or was a mega relief. 'So this Agar is one of the carapaces Blake was building?'

Jesus H. When had B developed a fetish for butt-ugly?

Azrael stood in the open doorway, gazing out over the dark ocean, the night breeze ruffling his hair. 'Yes. Agar is one of the four that were being constructed.'

'Four?' Nina's smile dropped. 'Ereshkigal has sent all of the Four?'

Something in the dip in Nina's tone didn't sit well with Kira. The immortal who thought all this was a barrel of laughs was spooked, and that couldn't be a good thing. Kira glanced at Vail, who patted Rossiter's face absently, his gaze locked on Nina.

'There were four carapaces,' Az said to the ocean. 'It would seem a reasonable conclusion, now that we know one of them contains Agar, that Diresh, Tek, and Sora have followed.'

'Are they all as big a dicks as that Agar guy?' Kira said.

'Yes, they are rather unpleasant.' Nina frowned down at her makeshift nursing attempt. All her jumping beans had left her. 'The Four are the most powerful gallu in Kur, all servants to Ereshkigal.

You humans took the ancient stories and reinterpreted them, gave the gallu horses, and renamed them the Four Horsemen of the Apocalypse. Aside from the fact that the true Four would devour horses whole rather than ride them, the story portrays their depravity rather well. When they are together, they are, quite frankly, terrifying. Even Inanna feared them when they came for her.'

Goddess of war shitting her britches? Not exactly comforting. 'Huge dicks,' Kira whispered.

'I don't understand how it is possible they are here.' Nina dumped the sodden blanket and got to her feet. 'If they are indeed all here.'

Which they likely were, thanks to Blake and her build-a-monster-a-human-suit project. Fuck.

Hyperactive Nina was so much more fun. Kira missed hyperactive Nina. A lot. That Nina had things under control, or at least didn't care if she didn't. Maybe this nugget of information would make it better. 'There's some kind of . . . water . . . at the Facility. The Tier, they call it.' Oh much better, sparkle back in Nina's caramel browns. 'It was brought here by . . .' Right. Time to dump the A card. But it wouldn't roll off her tongue. She cleared her throat. 'The Syranians brought it with them. From their planet. Some god of theirs sent them –'

'Aliens?' Vail shrieked. 'Holy shit.'

'Language,' Kira said.

'Sorry, but wow.' Vail grabbed at his hair, bunching it in two fists as if he were trying to stop the top of his head from blowing off. 'There's aliens in the Facility? That's a real thing? What do they look like, are they actually green with enormous heads?' Way too much excitement was being shown over the ETs, considering everything else that was going on.

'Oh no. They have rather lovely heads, at least, one of them does. Doesn't he, Kira?' Nina declared, some of the energy back in her voice. She padded into the kitchen, leaving faint brown prints all the way across the timber flooring. 'That explains the odd energy coming off Eron. He is not human at all. Kira is enamoured with an alien. Your taste is nothing if not exotic.' She searched through an overhead cupboard, shoving pots and pans aside. 'So the goddess sourced a living god from another universe to give Her access to this world. Whatever She wants here, She is going to great lengths to get it.'

'That energy you speak of did not emanate solely from the alien.' Az leaned against the door frame. Could have been posing for a magazine ad, if not for the shredded shirt and flecks of Anzu's goop on his arms. 'The Syranians are in possession of mea stones.'

Pots clattered out of the cupboard, hitting the floor and bouncing around Nina's feet. 'Mea stones? There are mea stones here, too?' The laugh was back, albeit less teenage-girl giggle this time, more despairing mother of toddlers. 'What type?'

'Control. Dominance,' Az replied. 'They used me to train themselves in their use. The Syranians grew adept. The training was most rigorous.' He turned his face towards the night sky, but Kira caught the snag in his voice. And she wanted to tear Captain Nex a new one.

'Well, if they intend to control the Four, it is hardly surprising,' Nina said. 'And from Anzu's vision, it is clear they do so already. One of them at least.'

'Telbourne,' Vail said, scratching at the edge of the cheek coin.

'Okay, random.' Kira frowned.

Vail edged Rossiter's head out of his lap, making the big man comfortable before he used the wall to pull himself to his feet. 'On the news, it said there were similar riots in Telbourne. Could that mean there's another one of those gallu there?'

'Possibly.' Nina dabbed at Anzu's wing, and the non-parrot-thing squawked. 'My apologies, friend.' Anzu let off another series of clicks, and Nina nodded as if she understood fluent Click-ese. 'Yes, you are right, Anzu. The Four are hunters, through and through.'

'Hunters?' Kira picked up the fallen pots, gripping the copper handle tightly. 'Rossiter said he'd heard they were looking for something.'

Pulling herself onto the kitchen bench, Nina swung her dirty feet against the pristine stainless steel cupboards. 'It was why they were created. Ereshkigal's hunters. She sent them after my mistress, after their little misunderstanding about the throne of Kur.'

Misunderstanding? Hell of an interpretation. Kira had read the myth. Inanna had gone full take-the-throne ballistic on her sister.

Nina continued, 'And if Inanna hadn't found a way to substitute that imbecile of a demigod she called her husband to suffer her punishment, the Four would have been trapping the goddess of war's soul on this planet for eternity, and not Dumuzi's.' Nina banged her heels against the steel. 'Oh dear . . .'

Kira's gaze shifted between Az's back and Nina's off-with-the-fairies face. 'Oh dear? Don't oh-dear and leave us hanging.'

But Nina paid her no attention. The tiled floor was the only thing in her world.

'Is it possible that the Four could relocate Dumuzi?' Azrael stepped back into the room, the lights sparking green fireworks in his eyes. 'Is that their purpose here?'

Nina lifted her head. 'Anything, it appears, is possible.'

'What's bad about them finding that Dimi guy?' This whole thing was giving Kira a headache. She poked at her temple, trying to ease the strain.

'Balance,' Vail said, making his way to the couch on unsteady feet. 'It's always about balance, that's what the Maiden teaches us. New gods, old gods, it's the same. If they kill Dumuzi, then I'm betting Inanna has to fill the void. It was hers to begin with. Which means we have a goddess of war stuck on Earth. And if those gallu can trigger riots, then what will Inanna do?'

For the love of all things holy and those not so much. This was insane. Blake couldn't have known all this. Kira chewed on her lip, painfully unsure.

Nina laughed, all light and fluffy again. 'What a wise little Wiccan you are. I think I'm quite glad we managed to patch you together.'

Fuck's sake. Kira took a breath. 'So what are you going to do?'

Raising her sculptured eyebrows, Nina said, 'Me? No, no. This is a team effort. Vail will remain here with Anzu. If nothing else, Wiccans are fantastic at healing, and I'm also not sure that another Shift wouldn't pop those coins right off and leave us with one dead little wizard.'

Vail's eyes widened, and his Adam's apple bobbed.

Jesus.

Nina rushed on, oblivious. 'You, Azrael, and I are going to New Weston—'

Kira and Azrael went for synchronised-reply gold.

'No. Kira cannot go.'

'No way. Az can't go.' That was not the protest she expected to be making. It should have been more self-centred. *Hell no, bitch. Kira Beckworth is not chasing demons.*

'Kira, it is—' Az began.

Kira jabbed a sleek silver digit at him. 'Don't you dare say it's all right. I've been in your head, remember? You need a lot of therapy, dude. Bad shit happened to you.'

A high-pitched squeal rang out. Kira cried out, too, covering her ears, searching for the source of the sound. Nina held a whistle, and a far-too-amused smile on her face. Where the hell had she hidden that thing?

'There is no debate. The three of us are going. You, Kira, because aside from the fact that I'm quite sure Azrael would refuse to leave you on your own, your sister helped build these metal shells, and your lover has one of Ereshkigal's pets on a leash. You are right at the heart of things. And, my darling Kira, considering you shine brighter than any human should, I think that is right where you should be.'

# Eron - 48

Eron pressed his fingertips against the pressure point between his eyes. The worst of the tension sat there, a dull headache that had plagued him from the moment of the Bind. The weight taunted him, never shifting in magnitude, either to lessen or increase. Constant. He'd removed the contact lenses at the first opportunity, but that had brought no relief. This went deeper.

He suspected that Biotechnician Gwen Weylen understood all too well the discomfort that came with close proximity to Agar.

'Done.' She stepped back from the stainless steel bench that held Agar's heavily inhibited carapace.

His upper-body clothing had been removed to enable Weylen to make the necessary repairs to the tears in the faux skin, which were numerous. One side of his neck had been entirely obliterated by the talons of the creature encountered in the alleyway. It had not been viable to take the gallu out in public in the state he'd returned. Tamas had ordered that Weylen be flown in from the Facility immediately. Evidently, the captain and the Messenger had been so supremely confident that repairs such as this would not be necessary that they had not bothered to ensure that either Weylen or Blake had accompanied either of the groups into the outside world. Eron had been somewhat surprised to see Weylen walk into the domed room where the equipment and inhibitor-equipped cells housed the Four. He would have assumed that Blake would oversee such extensive works.

'I'll inform the captain that repairs are complete.' Weylen's fingers shook as she removed her latex gloves. She glanced at him, biting on her bottom lip.

'Did you have something you wish to say?' Eron had noticed similar such looks being sent his way at various stages of her work. Not the kind displayed by Clara. There was nothing nefarious or sexual existing in this woman's furtiveness.

'I . . .' Weylen clutched at the tools she'd just gathered. She took a tentative step towards Eron. 'Have you heard anything . . . about Blake?'

Eron measured his reaction, ensuring his facial expression did not betray his curiosity. 'I don't understand.'

The woman pressed her lips tight and seemed unwilling to continue.

'What would I have heard about the Technician?' Eron cursed his words as they left him. Let it go.

'Nothing. Forget I mentioned anything. You can advise the captain we are done here.' She busied herself with packing away the array of equipment she'd used for the repairs.

Eron glanced back at the door. This room was essentially a mirror of Tech Room Two at the Facility. Compact and heavily insulated. No one loitering in the greater room beyond the closed door would hear a word Eron said. It was evident something was wrong. That much was clear in the sweat beading on the woman's brow, the unsteadiness of her hands, and the ripple of fear in her eyes when, on the rare occasion, she made eye contact with him.

He shook his head, shaking off the irritating curiosity with it.

'I don't need instruction from you.' Eron levelled a glare at the back of Weylen's head. But she didn't turn to look at him.

He left the biotech to her devices, fists clenched as he removed himself from the room. Stupidity, being here at all. Eron's presence was unnecessary. The opportunity to rest while Weylen was flown in and subsequently began repairs – a solid eight hours – had been Eron's to take. But he'd not favoured the solitude, the time spent with his thoughts alone. Despite growing exhaustion, the ability to sleep was slipping from him. His slumber had been so intermittent yesterday that on waking he'd felt even more fatigued than when he'd laid his head down. An emptiness sat upon him, trying to force a way in. Undoubtedly, it was lack of rest that scrambled his cognition process.

Eron strode down a long hallway that connected the containment area to the living quarters. The hallway of clear glass offered uninterrupted views of the city, which was slowly sinking into early evening with a sprinkle of sparkling lights beginning to appear. Some had never been extinguished. Giant advertisements blinked on the sides of distant buildings. To the east, far in the distance, a blaze of orange marked the glow of a fire. Considerable in size, he surmised, if it could be viewed so clearly from here. Further unrest amongst the humans.

Captain Nex would be pleased with the news of Agar's readiness to commence the hunt once again. Though, of course, the Syranian leader would show no obvious signs of pleasure. News of the transformative creature Eron had encountered had unsettled the captain greatly, though the signs of his unease were noticeable only to one such as Eron. Someone who had learned to read the minute signals that preceeded the captain's mood shifts. Being the one often responsible for those ill turns of temper made Eron especially adept at noticing them. News of the encounter with the feathered preternatural being had caused the captain's arms to fold, his slender fingers to grip too tightly to the folds of his jacket. By

133

nature the Syranians were not required to blink to replenish the nonexistent surface moisture in their eyes, but it had been a necessary habit to form in order to render themselves more 'human' and had become instinctual.

The captain did not bother himself with such trivialities while Eron had recounted the run-in with the creature. His eyes had remained wide open, as watchful as the bird-beast's had been. A preternatural being with the capacity to elude one such as Agar had only added to the general unease, the disquiet that had begun when Tamas's guards had met with resistance at the isolated farmhouse outside of Beleiro. And had risen when Kira and Azrael had eluded capture altogether. Eron halted, fingers once again finding the pressure at his forehead. Recalling his disastrous telephone conversation with Kira did little to alleviate his tension. It should have been his glorifying moment, delivering vital information about her whereabouts. But just the sound of her voice had set his temper rising. His mind betrayed him with images of her interaction with the gallu, the intimacy of it on repeat. As if Agar's constant torment was not enough, every lilt of her tone, every breathed word, enraged Eron still further.

But at the heart of Eron's anger sat an ember of bitter truth. He had considered the volatile exchange at length and could not say for certain that he had not purposely sabotaged the situation, ensuring Kira would end the call before it could be traced.

A door farther up the hallway opened, and a woman stepped out. She wore a forest-green uniform, the dress of the Facility medics. Giving Eron a brief nod, she headed in the opposite direction up the hall, leaving the door ajar behind her. Eron paused outside it. The white-haired woman, the one they'd removed from the farmhouse, sat propped up by several bulging pillows in a bed, glowering at the guard who was clasping heavy cuffs around her wrists. Vicinity binds. The guard informed her that should she attempt to escape, a massive delivery of volts would pummel her system. And kill her.

'Well, I'd say the killing part is inevitable, wouldn't you?' She shook her head, and the assortment of clips in her hair bounced with the movement. 'What a fine mess you are all in.'

Eron had been informed by Clara that upon Reuben's bloody collapse, the white witch had been instrumental in saving the man's life. A life-preserving move he admired. Tamas might be many things, Messenger first and foremost, but Eron had always viewed him as a lonely soul. It was doubtful he'd reward the rescuer of his closest acquaintance with a death penalty. But more favourable to her survival was the goddess this odd woman claimed to worship. The Maiden. The information Tamas and the captain may glean from this orange-skinned woman was far too valuable to end her life.

For now.

The witch shifted beneath her covers, and her eyes landed squarely on Eron. He did not recoil, as perhaps he should have. It was not the Maiden he would question her about, if given the choice. This weathered, diminutive human had shared Kira's company. Eron ground his teeth, jaw clicking with the pressure. But if the woman noticed, she didn't show it. Her lined features held no contempt, no fear. Tired eyes brightening, the furrows in her brow softening.

'Oh my,' she breathed. 'You are wonderful.' Her frown returned. 'But what have they done to you?'

Now Eron found movement. Rushing down the hall, away from her deep consternation. Telling himself it was his eyes she referred to. Viewing the Syranians without contact lenses took some time to get used to. It was the lack of irises that disturbed her, most assuredly. The white witch could not possibly know of, or indeed see, the deeper emptiness inside, no matter how readily her gaze seemed to sink right into him. Finding his core.

Eron sought out the captain without further delay, took his orders, and set about organising his departure with barely another thought wasted on the bedridden woman.

## Kira - 49

No doubt about it. Maseratis were impressive. Kira was partial to the British racing green. Nina had wanted to take out the silver model but had been outvoted by everyone except Anzu the bleedy bird-lion creature-thing. It didn't budge from the stained rug in the lounge room, even as Vail fussed over the wound with some witchy lotion he'd made. It stank to high hell of burnt rubber and fertilizer.

It was almost a relief to get the hell out of Nina's house. Kira's nostrils couldn't take much more of the stench. But a couple of things were really shitting her . First, leaving Vail behind made her skin feel all crawly-yuck. Like locking a puppy inside the house and saying, *See you when I see you, fend for yourself.*

And secondly, they were in a car. A fucking car. No fancy-ass teleporting this time. Nope. The world needed saving, and they were going to drive to the rescue.

Because there was no other alternative. Apparently.

Nina was still spent, even after another few hours of shut-eye, claiming to be still pooped from her first Shift in megayears, and declaring that the recovery time was too extensive for humans . . . blah . . . blah . . . blah . . . Kira had tuned out after 'No, we will use human transportation.' It hadn't stopped Nina from taking thirty minutes to pick out an outfit, another thirty for hair and make-up, then an extra twenty hunting for the 'perfect' glove for Kira to wear over her prosthetic. It was fake leather, so that was yay, but deep mulberry in colour – gross – too small, and the tip of the thumb had a hole in it.

They finally got on the road just after lunchtime. Off to see if the world was ending in a luxury car. Three hours driving so far. Heading straight inland. Three more to go, according to Nina. She avoided all other questions about 'the plan' by claiming every fucking song she heard on the radio was her favourite and blasting it so loud a megaphone would have been useless.

'What about now?' Kira grabbed the chance to ask as some tune from some dead guy faded. 'Feeling up for it now?'

Nina managed to make condescending look hot, lifting an eyebrow as if she were peeling back the shimmering bolero jacket she wore. 'Depends what you mean by it.' Her deep crimson lipstick glistened as her tongue traced her bottom lip. 'Oh, I love this song.'

Bullshit. No one loved this song.

'Shit.' Kira pulled her shirt up over her face and sulked into the Jean Paul Gaultier T-shirt she'd swiped from Nina's wardrobe. Long sleeves, nautical stripes, blue and white with an image of Popeye and 'I love Gaultier' emblazoned on the front. Because why not? But Kira's sulking spot gave her way too good a view of how far the armadillo had spread. Hugging the top of her right breast. Tits were free. There was that much at least. Because the idea of a bra disappearing beneath the metal if it spread any further, kind of made her want to start screaming.

She pulled her head clear, clamping the material against her chest.

Everything about the car screamed expensive. The leather seats clung to Kira's ass better than her favourite pair of vegan-leather leggings, and if the interior didn't stink so much of dead cow, she would have given the ride a ten out of ten. Likewise, if the driver didn't flatten her foot on the accelerator every time the traffic lights changed from red to green, Kira would have scored Nina highly, too. But the handmaiden was, as they quickly learned, not only the proverbial lead foot, she was a lead-and-concrete-and-Telteriun mixed together foot.

But still, it was taking too damn long.

'What about now?' Kira had bagged the front seat, making Az and Rossiter squeeze into the not-so-ample rear. 'Could you Shift now?'

'Shut up, Kira.'

'Kira, for god's sake. You're not ten,' Rossiter growled.

And it was an actual growl. He'd come to when Vail had started bubbling crap on the stove and filling the house with morgue fumes. The look of disappointment on Rossiter's face when he'd woken up and realised this shit was real and not some crazy dream he'd been having, and that in fact the real shit had gotten even more insane with the arrival of Anzu, had been priceless. And hilarious. Like a surly meerkat sniffing shit. Hilarious. But her laughter had gone down like a lead balloon. These were the first full sentences he'd said to her in the hours since they'd left the house.

'I'm fucking bored.' Kira planted her sneakered feet on the dash. 'I've gone from fighting off grimalkin, teleporting, and reading a bird brain to sitting here listening to Nina do bloody carpool karaoke and attempt to make us all carsick with her inability to use the accelerator properly.'

'Would you like to drive?' Nina said.

'Low blow. Fuck you.' Kira stared into the darkness. Nina knew full well she didn't drive.

'Well, fuck you back.' Nina wasn't so much condescending now as pissed off. 'I'm doing this for your own good –'

'Our own good?' Kira said. 'You said you were exhausted.'

'Of course I am, you have no idea what a Shift takes out of you, but I'm more concerned about you, and Rossiter.' Nina missed the gear, and the Maserati didn't like it. At all. 'I need you alert if you are to be of any help.'

Kira let her feet drop from the dash, shifting in her seat so she could glare at Nina. 'Help doing what? By the time we get there, Satan will be sipping pina colada in a downtown bar—'

'Who is Satan?' Az said.

'Not now, Az.' Kira kept her gaze locked on Nina. She was wavering. Kira could see it on her face. 'Nina, come on. We'll sign waivers or whatever.' No wait. Better plan. Brilliant plan. 'Stimulants. Would that help? I mean we were essentially super sleepy, right?' And horny. There was that. 'Pull into a gas station; we can get a dozen energy drinks and chug them.'

Maybe the first Shift had screwed up Kira's brain. Maybe the copious amounts of sex afterwards was making her mush, but Kira couldn't shake the waves of dread that came every time she thought about Eron and his bad-bouncer buddy. The raw hatred on Eron's face, as if he were a flesh-eating zombie and the whole world was a slab of meat. If nothing else, Kira needed to slap him upside his beautiful head and see if he was still in there. He had to be in there.

Fuck, if he wasn't . . . the thought made her gag. Kira punched her seat. 'Nina, seriously I—'

'Kira, enough.' Big man was well and truly done. 'Just let her drive—'

But Nina was doing the opposite. She slowed the Maserati and pulled over onto the shoulder. Not quite slow enough, though, and they slid briefly as she hit the brake.

'Is there a problem?' Azrael grasped the back of Kira's seat and edged forward.

Nina shook her head and reached for the glovebox. She leaned her arm against Kira's knee, giving her a front-row seat to the twins that pressed against a black crocheted blouse. 'We don't need energy drinks.' She sat up, clutching a small black drawstring pouch. 'I think you could be right, Kira. About needing the stimulant.' Dipping her fingers into the pouch she withdrew a smaller, clear plastic bag filled with white powder.

'Tell me that's cocaine,' Kira said.

'It is cocaine.'

'You still love that stuff, huh?'

'My drug of choice.'

'I remember.'

Rossiter cleared his throat. 'As nice as the memory lane might be for you ladies, is this a good idea?'

Kira already had the packet open, pinky finger dipping. 'Even if it does shit-all to help with the Shift, it is still the world's best plan. You done coke before, big guy?'

'I'm not a monk, Kira.' Rossiter's heavy brow pressed down hard over his eyes. Not a monk, no, but Kira hadn't pictured him as a blow kind of guy. The things you learn about a person in a crisis, huh?

'Handmaiden, are you certain this Shift won't tax you too greatly?' Azrael said. When he spoke that way, it wasn't hard to believe he was a gazillion years old.

'The distance from here to New Weston is less than a quarter of what I travelled from that field I dragged you from to my home. And this time, I'm a prepared for the boost you'll supply, bright one. This Shift should be short and sweet, the effects on the humans should be minimal. With a little nose candy, they may be rid of side-effects entirely. I believe it is worth the risk.' She patted the steering wheel. 'There is also the fact that this car needs fuel in about sixty kilometres, and I didn't bring my purse.'

'Great, that's sorted then.' Kira whipped off the fugly glove, and snorted a line off the back of her metal hand.

'Seriously, Kira?' Rossiter snatched the pouch from her as she handed it to him. With a finesse that was both surprising and impressive, he rubbed a pinky full against his gums.

'Right, let's give it a moment for the drug to take effect,' Nina declared. 'Then we begin.'

Rossiter pinched his nose. 'And go where? New Weston is a big place.'

'Indeed.' Nina stepped out of the car. 'And I have a very large property portfolio, with homes in most of the major cities in this country. Let's just say, I was able to get into the market rather early. And I never sell.'

The property mogul led them away from the road and down behind the dilapidated warehouses they'd pulled up alongside. Azrael was last to join the huddle in the shadows.

'I'm concerned about Kira's safety if we undertake this Shift now.'

What was he? Her nanny? Concern was nice and all, but it was also kind of fucking annoying.

'Az, I'm good.' Kira grabbed Nina's hand with her flesh hand. Surprisingly cold. Nina, that was. Maybe she was bullshitting about being ready for another leap through space. But too friggin' bad. Time to go. Dry mouth time. Toe tapping, lip chewing, teeth grinding time. If Nina didn't take them now, Kira was ready to run to fucking New Weston. 'Let's do this. Come on.'

Nina squeezed Kira's hand and nodded, eyelids low and sultry. 'Hold on, baby. Let's go find your spaceman.'

Kira opened her mouth to say, *Don't call him a spaceman, he hates that*, and found herself taking a hurried breath instead. The world fell away.

Turned into an instant winter wonderland. Well, more like a blizzard.

Air white as bleach. And quiet as all hell. Kira wasn't sure she was still holding hands with anyone. She wasn't sure she even had hands. Sure as hell couldn't see them. She was a snow cloud. For all of two seconds. Then reality loomed up large and flat and grey. She was about to make out with a brick wall.

'Shit!' Kira cried, raising her arms and bracing for impact. Impact didn't come. Something softer, warmer, gentler did. Arms curled around her, clutching her tight against a firm torso. Somewhere behind her, metal screeched across brickwork, and then they were sinking down, the arms around her guiding her. Kira's knees hit the ground, and she opened her eyes. She knelt between Azrael's legs, his knees bent and pressed against her thighs, holding her steady. He was on his butt and the wings were out, creating a barrier between them and the wall. They sat in an intimate cocoon of metal and skin.

'Good catch.' She'd been in this position, with others, many times. Always naked. Kira scrunched up her nose, and glanced away from Az's jade greens. Even if Blake had given the guy an actual dick, the thought of getting hot and tangled with Az just didn't sit well. Kira would punch down a football team if they tried to beat up on him, but banging nasties? Nah. It just wasn't like that.

Kira had no inclination to bang Az. She'd been in his god damn head, lodged in his emotions. Felt every heated vibe of lust and longing he'd had for his lover. Still had. Those two would have done anything to, and done anything for, each other. And Az hadn't let go of that.

She wanted to cuddle him and say, *Dude, it's all going to be okay.*

Fuck this was a weird day.

'Thanks.'

'You're welcome, Kira.' Az relaxed his legs, and Kira scrambled to her feet. 'Are you well?'

'Great. Good. Yeah.' She stood up, surprised to find that it didn't take any effort. No heavy eyelids, either. 'As well as I'm going to get, I think.' Her teeth still wanted to grind, but otherwise she felt relatively fresh as a daisy. Nothing like the knockout of the first Shift.

Score one for cocaine.

## Tamas - 50

Tamas took the lacquered crimson tray Clara held, steam rising from the freshly prepared food there. He gave her a dismissive nod, bracing for the customary tilt of the head and lowered lashes that always unsettled him, before she click-clacked away from him. But Clara remained right where she was.

'Are you sure I can't do this for you, sir?'

'I'm capable of carrying a tray.' Admittedly she'd carried it as far as the Fours' containment chamber for him. His split-skin fingertips pained him. But now Tamas sought to enter the cell and speak to the witch alone.

'Of course you are, sir,' Clara cooed, touching at her immaculate tight curls. 'You are capable of far more astounding things. I didn't want you to be burdened by these menial tasks. I'm happy to undertake them on your behalf.'

It was meant to be flattering. Clara was unfailingly flattering. And Tamas despised her. She was a remnant from his mother's days as head of the Facility, but unlike Reuben and Nari, who had also begun their time under his mother, Tamas had never been at ease in Clara's sycophantic company. She would walk all over someone like him, or at least, the someone he had been – an awkward, stumbling, stuttering fool – in any other circumstance. Wouldn't look twice at him in the outside world. She was as much a pathetic addict as Kira Beckworth was, only Clara's drug was power. If he asked her, Tamas was fairly certain Clara would lick dog shit off his shoes. His mother may have surrounded herself with such people, but Tamas would happily dissolve them all the moment the goddess gave him his just reward.

Tamas turned away, hiding a flickering smile. He stared into the access screen inlaid in the containment cell door. With iris recognition acknowledged, the glass panel slid open. The clack of Clara's departing high heels as she crossed the wide expanse of concrete that would take her out of the chamber and onto the penthouse rooftop where dawn hinted at the horizon was drowned out by the raucous breathing coming from within the cell.

The woman – Leona – lay on a thin blanket on the concrete floor, snoring at a remarkable volume. Had been for a couple of hours now. Falling asleep almost as soon as they'd placed her here. Captain Nex had wanted her removed from the equation. Terminated. But Tamas refused. It made little sense to dispose of her so readily, when they had learned nothing of the goddess she purported to worship. An entity that had managed to gift her with the power to expel the utukku. It was quite simply lunacy to rush to destroy that, and so Tamas had ordered she be transferred into Diresh's currently vacant containment cell. Nex had accused Tamas of harbouring empathy towards the woman because she had helped him save Reuben.

Nex was a fool.

Tamas glanced down at the tray he held carefully so as not to spill the soup he'd chosen for her. Chicken broth with ginger. His own personal favourite when he was unwell.

'It's just soup,' Tamas whispered under his breath.

Coming here, soup in hand, was hardly a sign he felt indebted to the woman who had ensured the survival of the one remaining human Tamas gave a shit about. Captain Nex's proposal was absurd. Tamas slammed the tray down on the only available surface, a narrow stainless steel bench that ran half the length of the far wall. The broth splashed over the sides of the green bowl, and the water glass wobbled violently. Tamas rushed to stop it from tipping and spilling fluid over the inhibitor relay panel embedded in half of the bench's surface. Diresh resided in this cell when not being walked through the streets of New Weston on Bel's mea stone leash, as was the case now. The containment chamber, a sizeable room built adjoining the penthouse, was devoid of both gallu. Eron guided a recently repaired and restless Agar amongst the senseless citizens.

The white witch's snoring lost its rhythm. She sucked in a noisy breath and opened her eyes.

'Ah, if it isn't the little demon master.' She grunted, rolling onto her side, rubbing at her wrists. 'I believe I have you to thank for those silly cuffs being taken off.'

'Well, don't grow too comfortable without them. They are close at hand.' Tamas rubbed his thumb over the engraved surface of Enkidu's inhibitor bracelet. Traces of dried blood marked its surface, but he had refused to clean it after Reuben's collapse. It did not fit him well. If he were sweating, it would probably slide free altogether.

The woman propped up on one elbow, her hair a wild knotted mess. A purple clip with a red jewel at its tip loosened and fell to the floor. 'Oh, that's my favourite.' She stretched her arm to reach it and cried out. 'Maiden's laces, that smarts.' Leona sat up, rubbing at her shoulder. 'Feel like I've been run over by ten trucks. How are you feeling?'

Tamas stared at her. He'd just threatened her life and this was her question?

Leona didn't wait long on an answer. 'Well, I sure as hell hope you feel better than I do. How is that friend of yours?'

The words jumped from him. 'He is stable. They are transferring him to the Facility.' Tamas shut his mouth, grinding his teeth. What had possessed him to say that?

Nodding, Leona sniffed at the soup. 'Good, good. Can I just say, I'm sorry, real sorry, boy, that you're in a mess like this. The big players always have a bunch of us running around doing their shitty jobs, right? And you're getting a right walloping too; those beasts you're holding aren't too kind on the senses. No wonder you're a little touchy. I reckon you might be a nice kid, in other circumstances.'

Glancing at the doorway, Tamas pondered exactly what mind game the witch was attempting to play here. Nice kid? Had anyone ever thought of him that way? Hell, he wasn't certain he'd thought of himself that way. Kid. Or nice. And he was certainly neither now. Hidden within an AI, Tamas had shot her friend. In the head. To begin with, the memory had churned his gut. As had the thought of the state he'd left Blake in, at the goddess's mercy. But the panic had eased, the sickened feeling falling away with each hour that passed.

'No. I'm not sure I'm a nice kid.' Tamas traced his bandaged fingers over the cast around his wrist. The scattering of utukku within him fluttered like rampant butterflies.

Leona's eyes didn't leave him as she picked up the spoon. 'Well, we are what the world makes us.' She gestured to his fingers. 'That's gotta hurt, huh? I could probably put together a salve –'

'Enough,' Tamas snapped. The niceties were growing intolerable. This woman was every inch  the fawner that Clara was. Saving Reuben, she had sought to save herself. She didn't care if Tamas's fingertips stung like they were dipped in acid. Or that his head held a constant ache now.

Leona took a long, slow slurp of the soup. 'Wonderful broth. Good choice.'

Not a single soul around him cared how Tamas felt.

'Enough!' Tamas rushed at her, slapping the bowl from her grasp, and clamping his hands around her head before she'd had a chance to swallow. 'I am Messenger to the goddess Ereshkigal; you will not patronise me.'

She attempted to answer, but the broth caught in her throat and she coughed and gurgled in his grip. The yellow fluid spilled from her lips, and veins in the white witch's throat strained beneath her orange skin. The fierceness of Tamas's own grip surprised him, and fuelled him. The roar of pain that came with pressing his damaged fingertips against her cheekbones flooded his body, and deep-set rage unfurled. Rage the utukku appeared to be starved for. Their motion within him was now turbulent as a summer storm.

'Tell me of your god. Who is the Maiden?' His spit landed on her face, and her body jerked, almost pulling her from his grasp.

'How did you repel the utukku? I swear I will destroy you all if you ruin this. Every last one of you. You are nothing. Saving Reuben will not save you, you stupid cow. You should not have messed with what is mine. And Azrael is mine –'

Leona coughed, and a smile curled her lips. 'Oh my boy, he is not yours. Or your god's. The bright one is all hers.'

'Hers?' Tamas tightened his hold. 'The Maiden's? Tell me more of her—'

A strangled laugh. 'Show me yours and I'll show you mine.' Dribble ran from the corners of her mouth. 'But I'm not sure I could tell you about the Maiden, not anymore. Whatever you've done in that place, things are changing. An old fart like me can barely keep up. But I think you know how awry things have gone, otherwise you wouldn't have crawled out of your hole to be here.'

Tamas sucked in a breath, ready to hammer her with another question, when all at once every drop of air rushed from him. Within, the utukku held perfectly still, their presence barely registering at all. The ringing in his ears vanished, replaced with heavy, laden silence. Leona's mouth moved, her eyes locked on him, but nothing reached Tamas. He let his hands fall from her face, and Leona slumped down onto the concrete, chest heaving. Spitting noodles and blood. Tamas clutched at his head. Deep, drowning silence sucked at him. The utukku moved in one enveloping wave from his core, sweeping out into his legs and arms.

Firing, it seemed, every neuron in his body. Setting his bones humming.

The bloodhounds had picked up a scent.

The silence imploded, and Leona's voice reached him. 'You all right, boy? Look like you've seen a ghost.'

Tamas's smile rose at her choice of words. Kira was the walking dead in so many ways. His skin prickled, charged with the utukkus' heightened energy. They sought release, straining beneath his flesh. 'Not a ghost, not yet anyway.'

A shadow crossed the white witch's face, her pallor no longer so offensively orange. 'You don't need to do anything nasty now.'

Tamas nudged the fallen soup bowl with his sneaker. The shoe had been pristine white not so long ago. 'Well, that will be up to Kira, won't it?'

The witch wasn't quick enough to hide her surprise. And it mirrored Tamas's own. Kira was close, unbelievably so. Right here within the borders of New Weston. His heart thundered beneath the vibrations of the utukku.

Leona stared up at him through strands of snow-white hair, her smile wide and her teeth faint yellow. 'Good luck with that. Go ahead, try to hurt her.' She chuckled. 'He'll eat you for breakfast, and I'll be handing him the salt and pepper.'

'He?' Tamas stared down at her.

Leona didn't answer, but then, she didn't need to. She chewed at her bottom lip as though she wanted to devour it entirely. Little wonder. Her mouth had betrayed her more than once already.

*The bright one is all hers.*

It dawned on him that the witch had spoken of Kira. Not the Maiden.

And the fire in her eyes just a moment ago told him it was no small bond. If Kira was here, then so was Enkidu. Tamas might have laughed at the insanity of it all if the incessant movements of the utukku were not forcing a grimace to his face. Kira Beckworth, the screw-up, the daddy-killing pain in the ass, had somehow become Enkidu's new Gilgamesh. But it was there, in the footage taken by the grimalkin. In the way Kira had reached for him. Tamas had just been too blind to see it, too utterly uncomprehending of the idea that the smart-mouthed bitch might be anything more than the nothing she was.

Tamas lifted the edge of his cable-knit sweater, finding the communicator at his waist and summoning Clara to his side. She appeared at the main doorway in an instant, and the clip of her heels came at a hurried pace as she raced across the chamber to where he still stood in Diresh's cell.

'Sir? Is everything all right?'

'Kira is here, in New Weston.' Tamas's delivery was robbed of the cool detachment he'd intended by a sudden lurch of the utukku. Ereshkigal's bloodhounds were impatient. 'Prepare a vehicle. I want an immediate departure.'

Clara nodded, blood-red lipstick glistening under the harsh lighting. 'Whom shall I have readied?'

'I'll take as many guards as we have available.'

Her frown lived barely a second before her smooth expression returned. 'You are going yourself, sir? Do you think that's wise? I'm not sure that Captain Nex will—'

Tamas reached up, and his hand found her throat, curling around its slender girth, bloodied fingers holding fast. 'Captain Nex is not my superior, nor is he here to take my place.'

She whimpered, her widened eyes shimmering – with tears, or the strain of lack of oxygen he did not know, and did not care. But as dire as her straits may have seemed, Clara kept direct eye contact. 'Sir,' she gasped, 'it's dangerous. You . . . are too . . . important.'

Easing his grip by the slightest fraction, Tamas directed his glare down at Leona. The witch eyed him, her thoughts well hidden behind a mask of mandarin indifference. He shoved Clara away from him, the force of it causing her to stumble on her impractical heels. The sycophant was right. Too many variables presented themselves now. One of them knelt amidst spilt soup and flecks of noodles, clad in a ridiculous lime-green tracksuit. And he stood right by her. Shoving Clara ahead of him, Tamas stepped out of the cell. The door slid closed, shutting the witch in her prison of blast-resistant glass designed to contain the Four. That should be what concerned him now. The search for Dumuzi, and the guidance of the Four as they hunted him. Not this infuriating hunt for the goddess's lost toy. He was a Messenger. It was his blood that had birthed the Four into this world and would deal Dumuzi a catastrophic blow when the time came.

He was too important to risk running after the Lesser and the wild man.

It was time to find out if Clara would lick the dog shit from his shoes. Tamas slid the inhibitor bracelet, a deceptively delicate ring of metal, from his wrist.

'Clara, you said you didn't want me to be burdened by menial tasks, correct?'

Though she nodded, and her breath quickened, the perpetual smile finally slid from her face. Tamas took her hand. Her dark skin was clammy, and it took no effort to place the bracelet on her.

'Yes, sir. What can I do for you?'

Tamas brushed his fingers over her cheeks, cupping her face in his hands. She shook beneath his grasp, but her gaze held nothing but wonderment. Her breath came in short, excited bursts. Beneath his skin the utukku maddened, writhing and jerking like fish out of water. Sensing what he intended.

He gave her a tilted smile. 'This will hurt.'

# Blake - 51

Cym had told Blake her burden would ease when she was taken from the Orientation Room. And, physically, yes. The Syranian had been correct. The fire at her joints and the ache that consumed her had lifted, even by the time he had carried her across the expanse of the room. But whatever sordid thing held hold of her mind was not giving up so easily. As Cym carried her down the corridor and into the elevator, Blake wriggled and shifted in his grip. Searching for a sign of Perry.

*You killed him. As you'll kill others.*

That nagging whisper that carved a well-worn path in her synapses, the viper hiding in her skull, taunted her all the way up to level three.

And it appeared to be right. There was no sign of that darkened familiar face within the confines of the elevator, nor in the stark corridors. No echo of that lighter, gentler voice inside her head. So Perry appeared to be the next step in her delusional state. Blake was not only hearing things, she was seeing them now, too. And the dread etched into her. What would come next? Her father? Kira?

Either would rattle her to pieces.

A curious sound left her, a whimper that had Cym clutch her tighter and whisper encouragement. Hold fast, he said. To what? Was he even real? Blake tried to slide her hand up against his chest, sought to grasp at the solidness there, but the viper was ready.

*Watch him burn, watch them all burn. You started this fire.*

She curled her hand against her own body instead, wincing at the pinch of flesh around the splinter in her wrist.

When they reached level three and Cym carried her into the ward, Blake's eyes went to the room where Perry lay. Very much real. Totally reliant on the machines around him for the few signs of life that came from him. A chest that rose in a rhythm too steady for any natural flow. Eyes sunken, his skin no longer a robust sepia shade but a tawny, faded pallor, a tube tugging at the corner of his

159

mouth. The regular beep of his heart rate monitor reverberated across the room, assaulting her senses, each one forcing goosebumps to rise along her arms.

She kept her eyes closed for a long while after that. A nurse took her vitals, and she and Cym commented on the unfavourable readings they measured. 'Body temperature raised, a fever,' someone muttered. Heart rate dangerously high, though blood pressure was steady – odd, she noticed no sense of rapidity within her chest – pupils dilated, and dehydration levels of enough concern that a drip was inserted into her left wrist, just beneath the bandaging. Cym instructed the nurse to stay clear of the right, where the splinter was a dark shadow beneath Blake's damaged skin. Her flesh was scratched and torn around that slender piece of wood. She didn't recall touching it, but the specks of skin beneath her fingernails, blood-soaked tips, named her the culprit.

Her old friend Jeremy, the medic who had stitched up her palm, joined the proceedings and attempted to lift the bandages clear and take a look at his handiwork. The possibility of infection was raised, and the small team sought to locate a cause. It took a momentous amount of energy on Blake's part to struggle against him, but she managed to lash out, though her hand fell well short of the shoulder it aimed for, and the effort took her breath away. But her moans and mutterings brought about the result she sought.

'Leave it,' the nurse, a middle-aged woman who had been casting concerned glances at Blake from the moment she was

carried into the ward, waved Jeremy away. 'She's getting far too
distressed, dangerous in her current condition. We will allow her
time to calm. Organise some food to be taken ahead to level nine.'

She must have been his senior, because Jeremy didn't
protest the task set to him.

Some time passed in the ward, though exact minutes, or
hours, Blake could not fathom. She drifted, floating at the end of a
tether held by the void-maker, which skulked in its cave, hiding in
the dark down in her gut. Sending only whispers before it. But
clarity was seeping in. Edging in like a slow-rising sun. The
fogginess letting go, clinging only to the peripherals. The sense that
someone approached found its way to her. Blake turned her head,
hoping for a glimpse of . . . what? A ghost? An illusion?

It was neither. Gren appeared at her bedside. Blake had not
noticed his absence from his own hospital bed, but it appeared his
healing process was complete. Here was a face holding the rich
sepia that was so noticeably absent from Perry's own. Gren's fine
dark hair, with its traces of silver strands, was pulled back tight
from his face, held in a bun at the base of his neck in the common
way of the Syranians. Eyes not covered with contacts, the white
orbs caught the light. Bright. Full of health. He moved in that
flowing, feminine way that all the Syranians did, with a gyration that
confused human assumptions, though he lacked the swing of hips
and hold of shoulders that marked Eron out as the most
androgynous of all the Syranians. Eron drew the eye. Blake would

give Kira that much. The alien held a mesmerising illusion of vulnerability. Perhaps it was the sheerness of his features: the pale skin, the silver hair. Limbs so slender it seemed impossible that he'd managed – so far – to survive his pairing with the carapace Agar and not been shattered into pieces.

*Break him. Break them all.*

Kira had broken. Blake had tried to fix her.

*Did not try hard enough. You didn't put her back together correctly at all.*

Blake cried out, clamping her hands to her head, digging fingers into her skull. Her momentary reprieve, the brief clarity, disappeared once again. Cym shushed her, placing himself between where she lay and where Gren stared down at her as though she were a dissection on a lab table.

'Is she dying?' Gren's flat delivery suggested he cared neither one way nor the other.

'She is unwell, but not dying,' Cym replied. 'Blake is remarkably strong.'

Rolling her head side to side, Blake found some comfort in the repeated movement. Cym released her hands, flicked a finger against the IV drip, tapped some codes into the machine that controlled the dosage.

'Just as well, I suppose.' Gren again. 'They want her alive, don't they? Insurance if the Lesser manages to evade them much longer.'

Cym rose to his feet. 'It is not just Kira who concerns them. Eron encountered some resistance—'

'Hardly a surprise. Agar is powerful, and Eron is not the—'

'Agar was not the concern, not in this instance anyway. Another rose, a supermundane stirred by the presence of the Four, the captain believes. But it managed to evade even Agar. Caused some damage that has been tended to by the Technician's assistant.' Cym's eyes rested on her. 'But if greater damage occurs, Blake's skill will be required.'

'You soften too much towards her, Cym. Show caution.' There was not the disgust in his tone that Blake might have expected, like what she heard when the captain spoke to Eron of Kira.

'It is not a case of softening, but hardening towards ill-thought-through decisions. And that is what I see here, with bringing the Technician so low. Her skills may yet be required in our task. What comes after that, I have no concern.' Cym touched his hand to Gren's wrist and, with the gentle sweep of fingertips against skin, betrayed the intimacy between them. If that bothered Gren, he did not show it, the opposite in fact. His body leaned towards his lover as if magnetised. Blake's eyelids fluttered, and daggers played at the backs of her eyes. Would she have even noticed if someone looked at her the way Cym regarded Gren?

Truly, insanity was taking her if those sorts of wistful, wasteful thoughts plagued her. Yet, the fog had again peeled back, the whispers so faint as to be lost beneath the click and churn of the room. Her gaze fell on the drip in her wrist. A concoction of Cym's making flowing into her. And she wondered just how much of the liquid sought to hydrate, and how much sought to feed and soothe her addiction. His last elixir had not been without promise, chasing back the side effects she suffered from the Waters. Did he aid her now?

Gren's arrival heralded her departure from the medical ward. Her condition, the nurse declared, had stabilised enough to warrant transfer. Blake was laid upon a gurney, a strap fastened loosely around her chest and thighs, and moved between the levels once again. This time down to level nine.

Deeper. Drawing her closer to the Tier. The heat and sting beneath her bandages suddenly grew bearable.

One of three containment cells had been readied for her. A narrow fold-out bed had been set in the back corner of the cell, a space no bigger than her bathroom back at her townhouse. These holding facilities were a backup to those down on level eleven and not constructed with human inhabitants in mind. She was lifted from the gurney and onto a bed, too soft for her usual taste but far better than the unyielding glass floor of the shrine.

*Blake.*

The voice thundered into her skull. Blake cried out and sat up, the jerk of her arm so violent it threatened to pull the IV clear.

At her other wrist, the splinter dug deeper, the flesh around it red hot with inflammation.

At the foot of the bed, a watery image. Her eyes were playing tricks perhaps, the image of the shrine's shimmering walls tattooed into her vision.

'Easy, Blake, easy.' Cym leaned in close as he pressed her down, voice low. 'I have done what I can, but I dare not add any more of the serum yet. Your body endures far too much as it is. We must be cautious.'

So, his guilt still plagued him. He still aided her.

*Blake.*

Catching her scattered breath, Blake fought to regain composure. Which would have been a lot easier if Perry were not screaming her name. 'I'm fine. It's fine.' She could not recall when she'd last spoken a coherent word or two.

*Blake. Can you see me?*

It took mammoth effort not to glare at the figure who watched her. Yes. She could. But his volume would give her an aneurysm if he didn't tone it down. The wait for her hostage makers to leave the cell and move out of sight was long and torturous. But in the corner of her eye, the vision grew still, less fluttering and threat of dissolving. It drew into greater focus, though was still transparent. Perry, or at least, an image of him. A holograph perhaps, her rational thought soldiered through the madness of earlier. But quiet reason plied her with images of his body, lying perfectly still in the medical ward.

Gren ushered Cym away. 'More important things to do.'

He spoke of the hunt that Bel and Parator, Seder and Eron conducted with their unholy dogs. The carapaces were on tight leashes, but the strain, even on the Syranians' enhanced bodies, took a toll. A toll Cym was supposed to monitor while they sought their prize. A prize Blake had paid scant attention to. Too busy lusting after their alien technology. Not so different to her sister after all. Succumbing to temptations. A smile caught Blake off guard, and she wiped it quickly. Kira was a part of this hunt, and Blake had put her there. Another wave of sharp goosebumps swept through her body. But the void-maker and its vipers stayed silent. And Cym and Gren left her alone, the latter striding straight through the image of Perry.

Hologram or hallucination. Reason or delusion. A quagmire seemed determined to swallow her reality whole.

*Please, tell me you can see me, Blake.* Perry's voice – with the accent Kira used to go on and on about – rocked with panic. His mouth was open, speaking the words, but the sound was entirely in her head. *'Cause I'm losing my mind here.*

He was not the only one. Gritting her teeth, Blake hissed, 'Yes. I see you.'

Talking to hallucinations. Hardly a sign of a sound mind.

*Oh thank god. What is happening? What are they doing to you?*

Both reasonable questions, but not one she had answers to. She had done at least some of this to herself. Stealing Azrael, stealing further sips of the Waters. Taking Tamas's invitation to work at the Facility. Ignoring her own instinct.

*I am death, destroyer of worlds. Including my own.* Her own crystalline thoughts this time.

'How are you here?' Blake swallowed, her throat thick.

*I don't know, oh god. I'm freaking out. This is so bizarre. One moment I was at the pub, then I think someone attacked me. Dunno, it was black . . . then I was here. Stuck in my body. Couldn't move my mouth—*

His distress pushed the volume up until it was unbearable.

'Stop. Please. You have to . . . speak softer . . . I can't handle it.'

*Am I even speaking, Blake?*

'Loudly, but yes.' She frowned, pressing at her temple. 'I suppose it's speaking.'

*Well, you're the only one so far who has heard me. And I've done a lot of shouting, believe me.* Perry drifted in closer, and it was immediately apparent that not all of Perry was here. No legs. The apparition . . . hologram . . . hallucination, tapered off into indistinct blurs below his pelvis. *You don't look so good, Blake. Please, tell me what's happening. I don't even know where we are.*

'The Facility, level nine.' Blake pressed cracked lips tight.

*And you, Perry, are brain dead on level three. Have been for days.* He'd said she was the only one who had heard him. Then she was the only one whose mind was lost.

*The Facility? Why? Is Kira here?*

Blake shook her head. Kira was not there, which was exactly why Perry was. He'd been caught in a crossfire that Blake struggled to comprehend. And now he haunted her. The fever filled her armpits with sweat, and a headache played at the back of her skull.

I *don't understand what is happening to me, Blake.*

Something she could relate to. There was scant evidence of understandability here. A hologram made less sense than a hallucination. And if a hallucination was this powerful, then the Waters had undone her completely. Blake curled her fingers into a fist, and a torrent of blazing agony stretched from her injured palm up the length of her arm. She bit down on the scream; spit forced itself between pressed lips.

Perry remained in her cell, still talking up a storm in her head.

*I'm having some kind of fucked-up out-of-body experience, and I have no idea how I did it. I mean, I don't know how I found you. It just kind of happened, that first time. When they had you chained up, and that weird-looking guy was carrying you. What was with that?* But he didn't stop to wait for any answers. *Then I was back in the ward, looking down at myself. And I tried to get back in, I really tried. But I can't, Blake. I can't get back, Blake. But I knew you could see me, and I wanted to go to you.* The screech of his terror scraped her already raw insides, hurting her every bit as much as her

*busted hand, or the damn festering splinter. That's all I did, I just…wanted it.*
*'Cause there's others in here, I can hear them. And it's freaking me out. I don't*
*know how to get out of here. I want out—*

'Stop!' Blake pressed her hands to her ears, her desperation
for silence overcoming the pain of pressed flesh. 'Leave me alone.'

Perry's voiceless mouth opened wide, his eyes even wider.
And he vanished, leaving the cell as empty as it had been before
they'd locked her in it.

'Perry?' she whispered.

Blake curled up into a ball, cradling her aching hands against
her chest. The silence she'd been so desperate for pressed down,
coarse against her skin.

'Perry?'

Pipes somewhere above her creaked; the rumble of the air
filtration system remained ever steady. And creeping closer,
marching up from the depths, the whispers beginning to rise. Blake
stared up at the ceiling. Innocuous, dull concrete. Layer upon layer
of it. Fortified with steel. Blake's shivers reached a new, painful
threshold. For the very first time, the tonnes of materials overhead
terrified her.

Those layers had always frightened Kira.

But she'd still come when Blake had called.

The fresh air and warmth of the sun, things Blake had given
such little time to over the years, seemed unfathomably distant. Far
too late, she realised how desperately Kira must have wanted to see

her, if she came all the way down to level eleven when Blake summoned her. The day Azrael arrived. Kira had been drunk, certainly, but loathed the confines of this place like no other. Little wonder. She'd died here. And never quite came back to life. But still she had come.

Blake's gaze fixed on a crack in the concrete, her mind searching through her own fractures, struggling to recall the last words she'd uttered to her sister as she'd shoved her out the door with Azrael. And for the life of her, she could not remember if she had said thank you. And be careful.

## Kira - 52

Azrael rocked onto his knees, using the wall he'd saved Kira from to pull himself upright. His wings curved into their hidey-holes on his back, yet another shirt ripped to smithereens. The guy was going to run out of clothes fast if he this kept up. And they'd left all the bags in the car. A distinct disadvantage to Shifting was lack of storage space. Kira searched for signs of Rossiter and Nina.

Touchdown was in an empty schoolyard. Kira and Az stood on a basketball half-court, where a single pathetic globe over the net did its darnedest to throw some light. The sky was darker than it had been a second ago . . . an hour ago? Fucked if she knew how long a Shift took or what time zone they were now in. A low groan drew her attention to a dark shadow just right of the brick wall.

'Rossiter, you okay?' Kira said.

Heading over to the lump, it was clear the giant bulk of Samoan-Canadian manhood hadn't been quite so fortunate with his landing. No one had been there to stop him from face-planting.

'Just great.' He spat out a mouthful of blood, his upper lip rich with it as it ran from his nose.

'Well, I did tell you to brace.' Nina appeared from around the side of the wall. The lengths of her dark hair, normally magazine perfect, were tangled as though she and Rossiter had banged nasties again, not portalled across the country. Nina cupped her hands beneath her breasts and made an adjustment to their seating position, making the girls bounce. With thigh-high boots coating her slim-fit jeans, the woman had made sure she looked fucking incredible for the end of days. 'How is everyone? All in one piece? Kira certainly is. Azrael, that was an admirable display of flexibility.'

'Kira was slipping,' Azrael replied, his words tight. 'I was required to do something.'

'And indeed you did. You had every limb wrapped around her. That girl was not going anywhere.' Ninshadur swept past him, running her hand across his chest. Azrael tensed, gaze fixed on something super interesting on the ground. 'She feels good, doesn't she? And I must say, you make quite the handsome pair. Perhaps when this is all over, we could have some fun, just the three of us. If you don't mind sharing.'

'Oh god, seriously?' Kira said. 'Call me old-fashioned but I'm not big on fucking on asphalt, in a kids' school playground.' A lie. She'd take Nina anywhere she wanted. Az might not be ringing Kira's bells, but holy shit just looking at Nina was making her damp. Fuck. Post-Shift horniness was a giant pain in the ass. Focus. Concentrate.

'Where is this house of yours, Nina?' Rossiter wiped his mouth on his shirt sleeve, leaving a blot of black on the deep blue material. 'We need to keep moving.'

'Oh, it's about two blocks that way.' She waved her hand vaguely towards south. 'I didn't think it would be wise to Shift into the interior of a house. Might end up lodged in a wall, which wouldn't be any fun.'

Rossiter led them out of the schoolyard, and Kira's thoughts bounced to Vail. This was where the little guy should be. Worrying about study and boys, and having his head shoved down toilets by assholes. Not wondering about how long some coins were going to keep him alive and if his witch foster mommy was trussed up like a turkey, being tortured by extraterrestrials and ludicrously buff demons in metal shells.

New Weston might have been having issues with riots, but there was no sign of it in this part of town. Every house along the tree-lined street was double storey and sitting on wide, unfenced blocks with perfectly manicured lawns and gardens that would have been breathtaking, Kira was sure, if you were into leafy green things. All the streetlights were working here. Nice and bright and shiny, though they weren't really needed. A dawn sun peek-a-booed.

Nina swept up beside her, hooking her arm through Kira's. 'Walk with me a moment.'

'Oh, I had a choice?'

Az and Rossiter strode ahead while Nina stopped to take a look at a cherry blossom in someone's front yard. Kira tried to pull away, but though Nina might look like fine china with a pussy, she was ox-strong.

'Do you know of Enkidu's past, Kira? Specifically a man he loved. Gilgamesh? A king actually.'

'Yeah, it's all history.' Badda-boom. Try the veal.

'Such a clever girl.' And such a condescending smile resting on Nina's lips. 'I just find it fascinating. The way he looks at you, well, it is astoundingly similar to how he used to look at his lover.'

'There's the difference then. Not lovers.' Even saying it left a weird taste in her mouth, like she'd bitten down on aluminium foil.

Nina ran her hand up the length of the glove covering the armadillo. 'No. And perhaps that is what bonds you. Both of you long for another, and know the great pain of terrible loss.'

Kira didn't long for Eron. Didn't ache at all over the guy. Nope. Crazy immortal bitch knew nothing. 'Fuck's sake,' Kira said. 'Promise me you'll never become a counsellor.'

'Tried it in the seventies. Not my thing.'

'No shit.' Kira so didn't want to just carjack someone right now and comb the city looking for a silver-haired alien. The handmaiden was showing her age, signs of dementia. Totally delusional.

Nina unhooked her arm from Kira's. 'Let's hope your story with Eron does not conclude the same way as Enkidu and Gilgamesh's. Theirs was rather tragic, broken hearts, broken bodies, long drawn-out illnesses and crippling loneliness.' Nina stopped dead. 'Oh, here we are. This is my place.'

Kira, still reeling from the grim summary of Enkidu and Gilgamesh, took a second to follow Nina's pointed finger.

Three storeys, all rectangular angles and long, wide windows, with wood panelling dominating the interior. Soft pearl light emanated from a room on the bottom floor and two more on the second floor. Circular lights built into the driveway marked the curve of the road leading up to the property. A high black iron fence surrounded the whole sparkling thing. Nina punched in a code, and the gates swung back with a slow flourish. 'I have no idea of the state of this place; must be two years since I've dropped by. A management company takes my money and promises me it's all being taken care of. I guess I'll find out.'

Safe guess to say yes, all was being taken care of. The low hedge tracing the driveway had been trimmed to within an inch of its topiary life in a variety of shapes – triangle, cube, orb – leading them up to a garage. Six oak-panelled doors were set into the design. The sloped roof and edgy black metal walls screamed, *A pompous architect designed me.*

'We'll go in through the garage,' Nina said. 'I want to check on my babies.'

Nina stared into a security panel alongside the first door. Iris recognition evidently. The oak panel lifted, revealing a white BMW. Her babies, as it turned out, didn't shit their nappies and burp milk.

'Boring,' Kira declared. 'What's behind the next door?'

She pushed past Nina, moving into the garage. It was lit up like a funky bar, that soft gold light just low enough to set the chilled-out mood. And it was a fucking vehicular candy store.

'Jesus,' Rossiter breathed. 'Is that a Bugatti Veyron?'

'No idea.' Kira shrugged. 'But that is most definitely a canary-yellow Lamborghini, and I need to be inside it. Right now.'

Nina obliged, and for the next twenty minutes, Kira and Rossiter creamed their respective pants, moving from car to car. Az was the least interested of them all. He stood by the open door, gazing out at the empty street down the bottom of the drive. But Kira and Rossiter played with the engines, revving the shit out of the things and moving to the next. Kira might not drive, but that didn't mean she didn't appreciate a very, very nice chassis when she saw one. Perhaps the coke was still in her system, because she was buzzing like a vibrator on high.

'So much pretty.' Kira honked the horn on the McLaren she sat in. The sound in the enclosed space was brain shattering, but even

Rossiter didn't complain. Too busy feeling up the wheel of the Bugatti. 'You love you some car, huh?'

'Makes the world less ugly if you surround yourself with beautiful things.' Nina opened the passenger door and slid into the red leather seat alongside Kira, wiggling her butt and smiling. But the grin was short-lived, sliding from her face. At the same time a shiver raced up Kira's flesh arm, while deep warmth spread up from her metal fingers.

'What's happening?'

Nina shushed her, her attention still on Azrael. 'Enkidu?' Her voice was not much above a whisper.

Az's fingers curled into fists, and he tilted his head, a dog picking up a scent. Now full-on goosebumps marched up Kira's sound arm. Whatever he was sensing, he didn't like it one little bit, and his trepidation weighed on her. Rossiter slowly got out of the Bugatti, searching between Az and Nina. 'Do we need to leave?'

'Yes.' Azrael turned and ran back into the garage, stopping barely a pace away from Nina where she stood alongside the McLaren. 'Do you command any edimuu?'

'No.' Nina shook her head. 'Not since the casino, and you know better than I do how disastrous that attempt was.'

Seriously? Nina was behind the waitresses-from-hell debacle? One day, when they sat down for a cocktail when all was said and done, Kira intended to let Nina know just what she thought of being strangled by possessed hotel staff. But not now. Now the air was tinder dry with tension. She was afraid to breathe too deep in case it sparked something. Her body ran heavy with alternate shivers and rushes of heat. Whatever was happening, it was fucked up.

'What do you –' Nina gasped, her deep browns widening. 'It is not edimuu you sense. Those are utukku that approach.'

'Take us from here, handmaiden,' Azrael demanded. 'You must—'

'I cannot, it is impossible so soon.'

Hauling herself out of the car, skin a mess of goosebumps and sweat, Kira shouted over the sleek red roof, 'What the hell is an utukku?'

Her answer came a breath later. The car alarms erupted, shattering the air into tiny pieces.

## Eron - 53

The regular thud of the helicopter's blades provided a relaxing tempo as they flew out over the western suburbs. It was early evening, and even this far from the city's heart, lights brightened the landscape. Trails of vehicles lined the roads, humans returning from work or leaving for an evening's entertainment. Eron settled his head against the headrest, allowing his eyes to close. If he were one of those mundane creatures, he would choose to sleep.

*Unsettled, are we, Eron?*

Eron did not bother to open his eyes to address the gallu seated beside him. Agar was bound at each wrist by a heavy Telteriun cuff, inlaid with inhibitor tech coded to his individual carapace. But Eron had him restricted rather than completely contained; it made for a more rapid offloading when they reached their destination. The gallu's thoughts could flow freely, something the creature took clear delight in.

'Likewise. The flying beast overcame you. That must stir some resentment. I believe it stirred some fear also.'

When the silence stretched out, Eron opened his eyes. Agar regarded him with a twisted smile, burdening the unfortunate features of the gallu even further. Agar tilted his head, eyes drifting to the window, fingers drumming an unsteady beat on the armrest. The lighting shined against the skin of his bald head.

*Fear, as with all emotions, is not one I am hindered by. You mortals of flesh and blood share that burden, Eron.*

Agar played at the mea stone Bind, teased at it, sending hot sparks of recoiling energy against Eron's control.

'Enough.' Eron sent the energy thundering back down the connection and was rewarded with a bare hint of surprise. Not on Agar's face, of course, there was nothing there but granite resolve, but in the tremor that ran through the Bind, vibrating like a guitar string plucked before stilling. Eron stared down at the ever-widening yards that surrounded generously proportioned houses. The greater the wealth the humans gained, the further they distanced themselves. Fences grew higher, gates barred the way forward.

They flew on in silence for another twenty minutes before the aircraft began to dip lower. A white sprawl of interconnected buildings drew into focus down below – the hospital Agar had been so intent on reaching the day before and had nagged at Eron to visit so incessantly this evening that he'd finally relented. If this were any more than Agar's bloodlust, he would be surprised.

The mea stone embedded in Eron's arm vibrated with uncomfortable intensity as the Bind bristled. Eron glanced at the gallu. He held his broad shoulders rigid, his face up close to the window, his chunky fingers clutching at solid thighs. The pilot set down the aircraft with a barely perceptible thud on the overgrown grass.

*And they have sent target practice to welcome us. How thoughtful.*

Eron followed Agar's line of sight until he saw a small white hatchback, headlights dancing as it travelled along an unsealed service road that hugged the property boundaries. Pulling up a short distance from the helicopter and its lazily rotating blades, two humans clad in identical beige uniforms, one male and one female, stepped out of the car and made their way across the yellowing grass.

Agar heaved at the Bind, a dog desperate to be let off the chain, but Eron countered him by pulling back hard enough to clarify there would be no such release. The effort caused veins in his neck to strain. They exited the aircraft, Eron bending low to ensure his long frame stayed far from the rotating blade. Agar strode ahead of him, the bulge of his biceps not affording him the luxury of being able to hang his arms directly by his sides.

'Hey, you can't land that thing here.' The male security guard was spindly, undernourished, with dark brown skin highlighted by hair bleached to within a shade resembling Eron's own. 'Unless you're with the police or military. That apply to you?'

His voice grew overly loud as the pilot raised the helicopter back up into the sky, taking the growl of its engines with it.

'No. It does not.' Eron placed his arms behind his back. The openness of the stance oftentimes assisted in reducing human stress levels. Writing on the side of the vehicle denoted it as belonging to hospital security.

'This is a quarantined facility.' The woman, hair shaved down to a hush of black shadow on olive skin, stood with her hands on her hips. Fingers hovered within touching distance of a gun at her right hip. 'We're going to have to ask you to shut down the aircraft and come with us.'

Quarantined. Eron's interest narrowed his eyes. Though illness was an expected side effect of the Fours' presence among the humans, so far there had been little hint of any major outbreak. Perhaps human authorities were more adept at concealing such outbreaks from their citizens than they had imagined. But radiance-wrought illness would not affect Dumuzi. Did Agar simply indulge his bloodlust? Yet again?

Agar let out a sound that might once have been laughter before it was chopped and diced into something far less hospitable. Perhaps it was that unpleasant sound that set these humans on edge, especially after hearing whispers amongst the authorities of flying beasts and magic. Whatever it was, something in their demeanour changed. They exchanged the briefest of glances before the male reached for the radio at his waist, and the woman slid her handgun from its holster. Radio at his lips, the man had no chance to utter a single word before he slammed it hard against his face. The blow was so fierce it knocked him off his feet, flat onto his back. Agar gave no indication he had done anything at all, no movement, no more laughter, but against Eron's flesh the mea stone hummed with the release of telekinetic energy.

'Jesus, Bauer,' the woman cried out. She still had the gun levelled at Eron, but there was no disguising the fierce shaking of her hands. 'Bauer?'

But her friend would not be answering her anytime soon.

'Lower the gun,' Eron said, arms still at ease behind his back.

'Not going to happen, buddy.' The woman jerked the gun towards them both. 'Both of you, raise your hands.'

'I'm afraid that isn't going to happen. Buddy.'

Eron breathed in, then exhaled and relaxed his hold on the Bind. Agar's fervour spilled out in a palpable rush against Eron's senses. The gallu released his wings, unfolding them from the storage cavity at his back. This was Eron's first sighting of the

183

appendages. When one sought to remain undetected, sprouting wings was hardly the most suitable course of action. But Agar had abandoned all pretence of normality here. The reason was quite simple. He desired to kill these humans.

Eron watched from behind the expanse of metal pluming from Agar's back. The woman dropped to her knees, releasing the gun at the same time, not a shot fired. Her agonised grunts, her contorted features told Eron that her actions were her own. Reason dictated he should stop this. Reel in the gallu. Keep control. Eron sighed into the heat emanating from the mea stone, penetrating his fibre, easing the tension he carried. He let Agar's violence fill him, absorb him, take hold of his blood and rush through him. Did not fight it, nor want to. At this moment, this tiny space in time, Eron could handle no more reason.

Agar's wings were vastly unlike the silken feathers of the creature they had encountered. His were voluminous strands of thin piping, all cut and curved to resemble solid wings. There was little elegant about their movement, jagged and harsh, much like the metal itself tearing a hole in the faux skin of Agar's back. But there was little doubt of the precision with which Agar could wield them. He swiped down, taking off both the woman's hands. She stared in silent horror at her appendages lying on the grass. Her silence weighed down on the moment, cloaking it in something deeper than darkness. But Agar was not done.

Eron braced at the jolt of strength shuddering through the mea stone. Agar shoved the very tip of his left wing at the woman's gut, impaling her on a razor-sharp point. Her eyes bulged. She opened her mouth wide, but her scream jammed deep inside. Not a sound escaped. Thin lines of blood ran from the corners of her lips. Sweat coated Eron's face, hung damp beneath his armpits, contrasting starkly with the dryness of his throat and mouth.

*Enough. End this,* whispered an infinitely small voice within Eron's mind. His own reason fought to surface but was easily quelled by the slithering, burning darkness that filled him. Agar still held the woman impaled on the end of his wingtip. Both of them were frozen, as if wrought in stone. The only movement came from the fluttering hem of Agar's black shirt. Not even the multilayered wings shifted. The guard was a limp weight of flesh, a fish caught on an impossible hook, no longer gasping for air. No longer capable of anything at all. And the sight of it sent sharper pricks of heat throughout Eron's body. Terrible, intoxicating agony. Agar retracted the wing blade. The woman's body flopped to the ground, face first onto the growth. Agar knelt beside her and dipped his fingers into the wound. Sensing the gallu's need, Eron coded in the release for the venting system that would unleash the radiance, Agar's own energy.

Eron was acutely aware of the speed of his own breathing. The rush of his pulses – and the effort it took not to sink to his knees and taste her blood as the gallu did. He watched the golden veins spread down along Agar's bare lower arms. The radiance spread through his fingertips, soaking into the blood and turning the crimson into something closer resembling a dying fire's embers. The gallu's broad shoulders jerked. He tilted his head back, eyes closed, mouth hanging open, caught up in the rush of release.

*Here. The demigod is here.*

Eron straightened, shrinking back from the bloodied corpse at his feet. 'In this body?'

Confusion muddled his thoughts. Dumuzi was reborn only into the sex of his original form. Male. And once found, Dumuzi's current human body must be retrieved intact, all his multiple souls still contained within a living carrier, not a dead and mutilated corpse. Fear curdled at the base of Eron's throat, chasing away the heat in his veins. The manic beat of his sex, the glands huddled at the base of his spine, steadied, slipping back into oblivion.

*There it is again, Eron. Your fear.* Agar's wings slid into the cavity at his back. *No. Not in this body. Do you think me such a fool? I know the gods' rules far better than you, pretty one.*

Eron blinked, the world brightening despite the darkness that hung around them. 'But he's here?' He gestured up towards the hospital buildings, still a good kilometre or so from where they had landed.

*There is little doubt.* Agar sucked at his bloodied fingers, watching Eron before breaking out the monstrous smile again.

## Kira - 54

Azrael hollered at Nina. She yelled right back, but Kira couldn't catch the actual words. Too much fucking noise to think straight, let alone hear complete sentences. All she knew was both Az and Nina did a weird synchronised turn-and-stare at her, before Nina shook her head. If Az had asked her something, the answer was definitely no.

'Then go.' Kira didn't need lip-reading training to catch Az's reply.

Nor did Nina. She jumped when he said jump and raced straight at Rossiter, who had his beefy arms pressed hard to his ears against the calamitous noise. Nina wrapped her arms around his middle; her slender limbs had no hope of making a full circumference around the big guy, but it didn't seem to matter. On contact, the air around them shimmered and blurred. Kira squinted. Were they actually fading out of view? She shook her hand, conscious that the armadillo still felt as warm as if she'd dunked it in a piping-hot bath. Fuck. Maybe all this shit – the Shifting, the warm and fuzzies with Az, the constant state of pants-shitting – had finally dislodged one of those connectors in her head. Neural points, or whatever it was Blake called the alien tech that enabled Kira to wipe her ass like a normal human.

Blink. Blink. Nope.

Nina and Rossiter were gone, the weird air still shivering, like a spa that just couldn't kick into full bubbling gear. So that's what a Shift looked like? Kinda pretty, in a the-world-is-melting kind of way. But Azrael wasn't about to have a chat about teleportation aesthetics. He strode towards her and grabbed her flesh wrist before she could open her mouth to ask what was happening.

'A little bit of explaining goes a long way.' Kira didn't fight him, but she made sure she sounded like she totally could.

'Ninshadur could not take you both, I'm sorry. You must get in the car, Kira. Drive.' Azrael pressed his palms on the hood of the car. The alarms fell silent. Nice party trick. 'Get as far from here as you can. Do you understand?'

'Nope. Not even a little. You're coming with me, right?' Ears ringing, Kira watched him work his fingertips against the car.

Drive? No fucking way. Vail was a half-dead zombie because of her last attempt. Her dad had been sent six feet underground the attempt before that. 'I can't.'

'You drove that vehicle before you were attacked—'

'And see what happens?'

'Kira, this is not the time. Get in the car.' Az's jade greens were drilling holes into her, and his low tone told her he was pissed – but no. Just no.

'No, Az, stupid idea, not going to happen. You have wings, dude; let's fly this one out.'

He gave her a sideways look, one Blake would have been proud of, his hands still laid flat on the hood. 'An equally stupid idea. I cannot defend myself and protect you, too. Go from here, Kira. It is not you they seek. But I can't outrun them with you.'

There was a grinding sound, a whir, and then the motor hummed to life. A deep throaty growl. The guy had a whole bag of party tricks. But then, so did she.

'I threw a grimalkin fifty feet.' Well, maybe a tiny purse full of tricks. Kira raised her metal hand, as if that would prove the point somehow. 'I don't need protecting. I can help. Tell me what's out there.'

Seriously, where was the bravado coming from? Maybe instead of horny after the Shift, she was just high. One lucky throw and she thought she was Superwoman. Never mind that the possessed waitresses from hell at the hotel had nearly strangled her to death, and all she'd done was slobber over herself. But, gosh motherfucking darn it all, if her instincts weren't braying like psychotic mules right now, telling her to stay with Az.

He lifted his gaze from the car, fixing his jades on her.

'Get in the car, or I will make you, Kira.'

Clearly not hearing her mules. 'I'm not leaving you –' But her foot-stamping tantrum would have to wait. The armadillo notched it up. Not just warm, but hot, hot, hot. Like *Fuck, I've put my hand on a hotplate!* type hot. 'Shit, what the hell?'

Goddamn it. This was it. The tech had truly lost its supposedly nonsentient mind. Maybe that alien asshole Captain Nex had planned it like this all along. The mother of all malfunctions. The armadillo swamping her, suffocating her beneath its reflectionless layers, eating her like she was the bean filling in a metal burrito. The thousands of minuscule artificial nerves frying her brain, while her metal heart just plain old stopped beating. Fuck, this was bad timing.

Her arm jerked, as though an invisible hand gripped her. Sweet friggin' Jesus. This was it. Kira braced. A gentle but firm tug sent her stumbling towards the idling white BMW.

'You must go, Kira.' Azrael stood some distance away and didn't look the least bit surprised or concerned that she was jerking about with her arm outstretched.

'Oh, Az, tell me you're not doing this.' She grasped at the door frame, using her flesh hand because the armadillo was in fuck-you mode. 'Az, this is bullshit. Stop now or I'll . . .' Fall into the driver's seat, apparently. 'Az, this is fucked.' Sweat tickled the side of her face as it fell down her cheek. Talk about being on fire, the armadillo was going to melt her. Every hair on her body, pubes included, bristled so hard she felt stuck with pins. He didn't even have the decency to look at her as he ghost-manhandled her while standing in the open garage door, his back to her.

'Az,' Kira shouted. 'You're hurting me.'

Az pivoted round, pinup boy features all mushed by confusion. 'Hurting you? I would never—'

What he would 'never', she'd have to guess. A stream of brilliant blue light snaked around his torso and pulled him backwards out into the darkness.

'Az!' Around her own waist, a sudden tightness made her catch her breath. If she had been wearing a belt, she'd have assumed it was snagged on something. But only her hips held up her faded jeans.

Sapphire light pulsed, blazingly bright plumes of light that made it hard to see straight. Kira stumbled from the car, Az's hold on her gone as suddenly as it had arrived. The goosebumps and the heat hadn't gone with it, though. Her T-shirt clung to her, the armadillo still baking her. But the cinching around her middle eased at least. Kira ran to the open doorway, searching for signs of Az. It was like trying to stare into a blue sun, painful as hell. Her eyes watered with the strain. Kira caught sight of an instantly recognisable silhouette in the cobalt Fourth of July explosions. And didn't like what she saw. Az was down, and the wings were out. Hovering way too close were two balls of light. She squinted. The balls weren't solid masses. Tiny points of light, hundreds and hundreds of them, made up the larger shape. Az swung a wing tip, catching the ball of light headed for his side. Mini fireworks this time, sending orange sparks flying when metal met orb and dampening the glare long enough for Kira to see him take a second swing. Not so great this time. He missed. And the orb took full advantage, rocketing in towards him. Just before impact, though, its shape altered. The individual points moved in unison, like a school of glittering sardines, shaping themselves into one long ribbon of light. The ribbon lashed around Az's waist.

Both he and Kira hollered in pain.

'Balls!' There had to be barbwire around her waist. Had to be. And Christ almighty, it stung. Kira pulled at her shirt, pressing her hand to her waist. Smooth skin, damp with sweat, not blood from open wounds. Azrael's agonised cries tore at Kira's eardrums, and her goosebumps got goosebumps. Shit. She and Az were doing that thing again. The weird voodoo crap that gave her a front row to his freak-outs. Only this time, it wasn't in her head. It was physical.

And it was hurting him big time.

Kira half expected to see flames shoot out of her fingers, her brain telling her that the armadillo burned red hot. But outwardly the metal was its usual non-reflective self, and a quick touch with a tentative flesh finger revealed a cool surface. The heat thing had happened back when Tamas's dickwads had attacked her with grimalkin. Righto. Time for a huge leap here. If she wasn't insane – and that was highly likely – then maybe armadillo got all hot and heavy when it was ready to unleash hell on dickwads.

'Bad idea, bad idea.' But Kira ran anyway. Straight at Az and his ribbon tormentor. Whatever that thing was, it was more than a robotic grimalkin, more than a crazed room service attendant, and probably not something she should be bolting at with only her good looks, charm, and wild ideas to protect her. But if the sardines didn't get their goddamn blue hands off Az, she was going to . . . fuck, this was such a dumb idea. Azrael wrestled with the blue binding, managing to wrench a portion of it free of his chest. At the moment it tore from his faux skin, Kira gasped. A hard spasm gripped her ribcage.

'Kira, stop, what are you doing?' The light gyrated in Az's grasp, and he threw his head side to side to escape its darting tip.

But she was a woman on a psychotic mule, and no damn cramp was going to stop her. Kira dodged Az's swaying wing, dropping onto her knees beside him. The points of light held their form and thrashed about like a lizard's cut tail. Kira grabbed hold with both hands.

'Jesus!' Kira screamed, saliva spraying into the air.

Mother of all fuckers. In terms of bad ideas, this one was a keeper. She might as well have just grabbed a handful of tacks. But she wasn't letting go. Not till it killed her. And that was going to be any fucking second now.

A wing swept right by Kira's face, uncomfortably close, and sliced right through the sapphire serpent. Pinpoints of diamond-bright light scattered in all directions. The screech that came with the contact might have freaked Kira the hell out if it weren't for the fact that she was pretty sure her flesh hand was melting.

'Kira? Are you all right?'

'Peachy.' Kira curled her hand against her chest, not keen on taking a closer look, expecting to see all kinds of nasty. 'Are they dead?'

Without the blue suns to light up the garage, it seemed oddly dull.

'Not yet.'

'Then what are you waiting for?' Kira rested on her knees, not entirely certain she wasn't about to puke. Her mule had well and truly bolted. Though her arm still kept trying to tell her brain it was heated.

'You appear unwell—'

'I'm fine. Go, Az.'

'You must leave here, Kira. Attention will have been drawn.'

No shit, Sherlock. 'I'll handle me, you handle those fishy bastards.' He frowned and she scowled, waving his question away before it was asked. The skin on her palm crawled, like a bunch of ants with spurs on their heels were traipsing about. 'The car's still running. I'll get out of here. You said they were after you. I'm fine.'

Bullshit award, right here, thanks. If the skin on her palm wasn't one big burn, she'd eat her too-tight sneakers. And her chest muscles still twerked and jerked, forcing her to take shallow breaths. Trying to take a deeper gulp brought a whole new bloody uncomfortable realisation. She wasn't about to take her shirt off right now, but it sure as hell felt like the press of metal had edged farther across her chest, down into the almost nonexistent valley between her tits.

Az nodded, his attention already shifting from her to the night sky. 'I will find you.'

He lifted off. A sight she doubted she'd ever get bored with, wings beating in slow powerful thrusts. Kira's hair danced under the shift of air. Az flapped his way up over the garage, and she lost sight of him.

Suck it up. Time for big-girl panties. Kira staggered to the car. Her stomach heaved as she forced herself back into the driver's seat of the still-idling BMW. The god-awful noise they'd just made was bound to attract more than just supernatural attention. It was a miracle the place wasn't surrounded by cops already. Kira pulled the door shut, swallowing down on the puke ball that was poking up her throat.

'Do it, K. Hands on wheel.' Problematic. She turned over her flesh palm, jelly hand shaking.

But the flesh wasn't one big burn. It was a mass of tiny pinprick-sized holes, some oozing drops of blood, but most just inflamed and angry. 'You're good. All good. We've got this.' At least armadillo, though warm, wasn't roasting her alive and, so far as she could tell, wasn't trying to devour her right boob. The goosebumps had stopped partying over every inch of her body , as well. Was that an Az thing, too? He'd sensed those things coming before they were anywhere in sight. If she could sense his pain, his fear, why not instinct as well? Either that, or her arm was taking on a life of its own. Which was also, at this point in time, a valid theory. Jesus.

Kira had no clue which of those options made her more nauseous.

Oh, this was just such a wonderful day.

'Drive the friggin' car, Kira.' She pressed her forehead against the steering wheel, staring down at her feet. Daddy issues were the least of her worries. 'And go where?' she asked her toes.

They didn't answer. She sighed and sat up.

The SUVs came out of nowhere, two of them flooring it up the driveway, headlights blazing, screaming to a halt in front of her only exit. People flowed out of the cars like an oil spill.

'Oh shit.'

How the fuck had they found her? Tamas's goons were suddenly everywhere. Black blobs surrounding her car before she'd reached for the door. A guy with a cultivated five o'clock shadow wrenched open the driver's door. Kira scrambled to try to clamber into the passenger seat, but one press of her injured palm to the leather and she was seeing stars.

The passenger door swung open. A blond guard she was fairly certain she'd slept with a while back leaned in. If he remembered it fondly, it didn't show on his pinched face.

'Hello, Kira. You might want to start thinking about how to call back the property you stole.' He patted at the semiautomatic hanging at his waist.

'You might want to start thinking about dental hygiene,' Kira said.

The punch was whiplash fast. Right on the jaw. A joint in her neck cracked, and the tang of blood seeped from a tear in her lip. If he'd really wanted to, he could have knocked her out cold. Asshole just wanted to spook her. Dominate her. Screw that. Kira licked the blood off her lip, slowly, without taking her eyes off his face.

'No sign of the asset, sir.' A feminine voice came from behind the balaclava worn by a guard standing to Blondie's right. He didn't acknowledge the update; he only had eyes for Kira.

'Boss wants to see you.'

Blondie was on her before she could tell him to fuck off, dragging her out of the car, and just as quickly shoving her into one of the waiting SUVs. Everything about this was black, the uniforms, the cars, even the interior of the car. Only the dashboard threw any light, and that was pretty pathetic. She might as well have been hurled into a cave. Took a second for her eyes to adjust and realise she wasn't alone in the cave.

'What the fuck . . .'

A woman sat in the back seat, skin dark as ebony, a shock of curls framing her face. Bloody rivulets traced lines down her face and dripped off her chin. She wasn't exactly smiling, but considering the fact that it looked as if someone had taken a million pushpins to her face, she probably should have looked less self-satisfied. Nice hair though. Oh to have curls that could be tamed.

'Hello, Kira.' The woman's voice wasn't as steady as the rest of her. Not by a long shot. 'My name is Clara, and I've come to collect you on behalf of Tamas.'

'Oh you have no idea how much that is not going to fucking happen.' Kira grabbed at the doorhandle, as if they'd just let her step from the car. No go. What a surprise. 'Let me the fuck out of here.'

'That is not going to happen. I suggest you come quietly. If you are a good girl, perhaps you won't end up like your sister.'

If blood could freeze, it happened in that moment. Even the armadillo's heat shrank away, leaving a trembling Kira ice cube. 'What have you done to Blake?'

'She is suffering because she would not do as she was told, Kira.' Liquid honey, laced with acid.

Kira launched herself at Blood-face, a choice stream of obscenities at the ready. But the woman was quicker. Kira didn't even see the Taser until it was filling her with a gazillion agonising volts.

## Kira - 55

If ever Kira had needed proof that Tamas was an asshole of the highest magnitude, then this was it. The tasering in the car by Blood-face Barbie had been bad enough. It'd made her piss herself, too, which was making for all kinds of discomfort in Crotchville. The chafing was going to suck. But that paled into nothingness in light of what Tamas was doing to her right now. Holy mother of god, this shit hurt.

'Ass . . . fuck . . . Jesus.' In her head those words were leaving her tongue and spewing up into Tamas's face, but she couldn't hear much save for the roar of blood in her ears. Her back arched, rising up to try to find somewhere in the room where her skin wasn't trying to rip itself apart. Though nothing bound her to the bed, Kira's arms were plastered down hard against the bedcovers beneath her. The mattress was ridiculously soft against her back, but just the brush of the material against her skin inflamed every nerve ending, sending liquid lava moving through her veins.

The fuck face was killing her. This was it. All over, red rover. Tamas, scared of his own shadow, mumbling, dribbling piece of shit that he was, was killing her. When Blood-face Barbie and her thugs had dragged her in here and thrown her onto the bed, Tamas had stormed into the room like a goddamn tornado, slapping his hands to her face and screaming at her to bring Enkidu to them. So, there was that. He knew about Az being the old wild man and all. But it had been hard to give a shit at the time. Tamas's skin had felt like acid against her own. And the pain hadn't stayed skin deep; it had found its way into every pore and raced through every vein. Radiation, maybe? A poison? Goddamn it.

Tamas leaned over her. The jerk seemed bigger than she remembered. More inflated somehow. Way more pissed off than she'd ever seen him. If she could think straight, hell she might have even been scared of him.

'You will bring him to me, Kira.' His pupils were way too wide, considering how bright the room was. 'Whether it is through your words, or your pain, it will be done. I know you have bonded with him, impossible and ridiculous as it may be. Let us see how deep the bond goes. Bring Enkidu to me, and I might let you live.'

As if to prove his point, the wild jerks and thrust of her body stopped. She was a sweaty, shaking mess, desperately trying to catch a breath before it began again. And it would. A person didn't look at you the way Tamas was if they didn't intend to keep hurting you.

'I don't . . . I don't know . . . how.' Kira's throat had been sandpapered; even those few words made her wince.

'Find a way.' Tamas couldn't have sounded more terrifying if he'd screamed it at her. He'd barely been audible at all. He leaned in closer. 'Enkidu may have destroyed most of the utukku, but I already have what I need. I have both his weakness and yours. Bring him to me, Kira. Let your misery guide him in. If you do not, understand that Blake already suffers. What you are feeling now? It is nothing compared to her pain. These utukku that remain in my control are pathetic in comparison. And for every hour, every minute you keep Enkidu from me, her suffering will grow. You should not have taken what doesn't belong to you.'

The words dug in, salty fingers in an open wound. She tried to throw something vile back at him. Even a glare would have been enough, but it was body-shatter time again. Fresh spasms ran through her. Hundreds of needle points poking at her insides. Utukku. Something living inside her. Kira screamed, her hips twisting to one side, ass bucking up off the bed. If this kept up, she'd break something or pull a limb from a socket. Of all the times it might be a good thing for the armadillo to go insane, now sure as hell was it. Instead, it was the only part of her that hadn't jerked off the bed. Her arm like an anchor, stopping her from launching entirely. Tears streamed, cool against her skin, running down across her temples.

Christ almighty, Blake. Her sister had looked like a skeleton walking last time they'd met. If Kira was close to breaking a bone, how the fuck was Blake handling this? Or maybe Tamas was lying through his teeth.

Or . . . maybe Blake was already dead.

'Cunt.' She spat. Her jaw spasmed, teeth slamming hard together, and the veins in her neck threatened to rip themselves free. Vomit smacked at the back of Kira's throat and flew from her mouth. She tilted her head, aiming for Tamas. Great idea, but the execution sucked. Most of it ended up on her own shoulder, soaking through the material of her shirt and onto the dull surface of the metal. The wild jerking of her own body sent her cheek slamming against the moist pile of gut wrench, and that's where it stayed as a momentary respite came. Even though her nostrils filled with the smell of her own vomit, Kira didn't have the strength or inclination to move. Barely had enough to breathe. Fuck, she hoped Az had made it really hurt when he'd killed those utukku things. Score one for the winged dude.

*Kira.*

Azrael's voice burst through her senses like a wordy migraine. Kira cried out. Holy shit balls. A full-on, proper word. Inside her head. And no one had mentioned telepathy didn't tickle.

*Kira. You are in pain.*

Volume, Az, fucking volume. If she had a choice, Kira would be clawing at her head right now. Pain? Hell yeah, thank you, Captain Obvious. Oh, shit. Captain Obvious was Azrael. Bring him in, Tamas had said. And he hadn't been talking about making a quick call. Shit. How the fuck had this dude known she had any kind of connection going with Az?

*I am coming, Kira, hold fast. The utukku have been destroyed.*

Yeah well, not all of them. It was official. Not one single spot on the outside or inside of her body didn't ache and pinch and burn like the fires of all holy hell.

*Az?* Tap, tap, is this thing on? *Don't. Don't come anywhere near this place.* Did he roger that? *Should she have done an 'over and out'? Az? You hear me? Stay away.*

Don't give the fuckers what they want. If Blake was alive, it sure as hell sounded like it was because of Tamas's hard-on for getting Az back. So he was getting jack shit. Kira groaned, rolling her head side to side. She thought she'd wished she were dead before. That shit had nothing on this.

The woman who had tasered her, Clara of the perfect curls, rushed into the room. Breathless, face clean now, make-up plastered thick on her face, lipstick glittering ruby red and dark kohl around her eyes. She paid no attention to Kira and her fresh coating of vomit.

'Sir, Captain Nex has just arrived.'

'Not now.' Tamas didn't stop his glare-fest, and Kira wasn't about to look away – even though her eyes watered so hard she was probably going to drown in her own tears before he rattled her apart.

Clara cleared her slender throat, adjusted the elaborate bow at the neck of her lavender blouse. 'Sir, we have to leave. Now.'

Tamas turned to her. She was panting like a porn star at the end of a take. And clearly was shit at telepathy. No word from Az.

'I don't *have* to do anything,' Tamas said.

Then, there he was. King of the aliens. Captain Nex stood in the hall beyond the open door. He glanced at Kira, eyes devoid of their contact lenses. Two great white orbs peered at her with utter indifference, empty of anything that might resemble giving two shits. Even if he was loving this – seeing her covered in piss and vomit and writhing in pain – then that didn't show either. The guy was more robot than grimalkin.

Couldn't have been less like Eron if he tried. Nex wouldn't have liked to twist her hair around her fingers because he liked the way it felt against his skin; the captain would have wrenched it out at the roots. The prickle at the backs of her eyes had nothing to do with whatever venom Tamas had injected her with.

'Come, Messenger. Now,' Nex said.

Hell, with that tone of voice, Tamas's damn goddess would have jumped when the captain said jump.

'The interruption had better be worth it.' Tamas made a weak attempt to sound just as threatening.

'The Lesser and the missing gallu are no longer your priority.' The captain flicked a hand at Clara. 'Have her taken to the containment chamber.' As he strode out of sight, Clara nodded so hard it was possible her head would fall off. Which would have made the day decidedly less shitty. Tamas didn't follow after the captain immediately.

'I want every available guard stationed on the chamber, Clara.' His attention returned to Kira. 'Do as you are told, and this will end.'

Kira opened her mouth, hoping to tell him where to stick his end. But her words made as much sense as those she'd dribbled in Nina's bed after the Shift. Holy crap, where were Nina and Rossiter? She could sure use a couple of knights right now. Armour didn't even have to be shiny. Clothing completely optional.

The door slid shut and Kira was alone. Her muscles took turns jerking and cramping, and her skin was damp with the sweat all the movement was generating. Warmth ran from her nose, thick against her top lip. A dab of her tongue told her she was bleeding.

*Kira, I must come to you. You are weak.*

Oh sweet Jesus, weak was the understatement of the decade. And what Az *must* do was tone down the volume. Still, aside from that, the hum of him inside her head wasn't entirely unpleasant. If nothing else, she wasn't alone. *Stay away, Az. Blake wanted you out of there.* Kira blinked through tears. Not cry-cry tears, but the type that come when you kicked your toe, and hit your funny bone, and jammed your finger in the door. Six million times. *She didn't want them to have you. Don't let me fuck this up.*

Did that already. Big time. Hell, this was karma if nothing else. Paying her penance for fuck-ups made.

*I can reach you.* Azrael's voice, as clear and familiar as though he stood beside her.

*I don't care. Don't need saving.* Screw the knights. Rescue was overrated as all buggery. She'd treated life like shit since the accident, why not die in a pile of it? Least this last hurrah might be worth it. Az, find Nina, find Blake. Bring these fuckers down.

Sweat mingled with the blood on her lips. Thinking was taking too much effort. Her synapses were coughing and sputtering like Leona's shitbox.

Tan Queen. Annoying as she may have been, man, it would suck if she was dead.

*Kira —*

*Stay the fuck away. I'll be fine. I've got this.*

Call her the queen of lies and hand over that crown of thorns. Kira's body screamed with the slice of a thousand knife cuts, each burning holes to the bone, the material beneath her a giant hot-water bottle. Fine. Do your worst, Tamas. Her skin had never fit right since the day they'd put her back together anyway. Too tight, too suffocating. Like that floaty thing inside her, a soul, a life force, whatever you called it, had been ready for liftoff that day she'd hit the tree, and it didn't like being sewn back together one little bit. Kira had died. Dead as a dodo. Finished. Sayonara. The end.

No one should mess with that. But they had. Blake had. Made deals with beautiful devils in exchange for a patchwork sister she never spoke to. And look at the shit pile they were all in now.

*Promise me you'll stay away, Az.*

But the angel had gone mute. Fuck. If that dumb-ass son of a bitch tried to get to her, she was going to kill him herself. One thing, just one thing Blake had asked of her: to keep Az away. And there had been a second promise made. One from Kira to Az. After his meltdown at Nina's. A promise to make sure he never got his ass hauled back to Kur. For fuck's sake, why was the world so intent on not letting her keep her promises? Of making her look like a dipshit incapable of getting anything right? Through the waves of hurt, something else rolled. Anger washed through her, sharp and decisive. Damn both of them to hell. For the first time since she'd awoken here in this bed, heat flowed from the armadillo. It rushed through her body, raising her body temperature to a new saturated high.

Just like it had before Azrael had gone postal on the Facility asshats attacking her. Christ. She closed her eyes.

*Az! Answer me.* Her own voice roared in her head. Stay away.

'Stay away!' The scream launched from her mouth on a rocket of pure rage. A heavy weight landed on her metal hand, and Kira's eyes flew open. 'What the –'

The entire room ignited. Streaks of gold and shimmering red flame plumed around her, rising as high as the ceiling and lapping at the walls. And at the heart of it, a tiny black mouth locked around her thumb. Bradley. At the heart of a firestorm, the slimy guy was chowing down on her prosthetic digit. A bite so pathetic it didn't register on her sensors at all.

'Bradley, what are . . .'

Wait. It wasn't just his bite that didn't register. Nothing did. The flames held no heat. And she wasn't being torn into a million pieces anymore. A few distant aches and pains, but nothing more. Kira sat up, and her bones didn't threaten to shatter. But Bradley wasn't done with his metal dinner. He clung there, beady eyes fixed on her. And the flames took shape around him, sinking down to wrap around him, a ghostly blazing shadow. It sat away from his body but mimicked his curves, growing him into something a hell of a lot more intimidating than a newt. This was Komodo dragon territory. A fucking dinosaur-shaped sun hovered over the bed, and at its heart, a black newt still clinging to her thumb.

Kira's breath caught as a vibration rumbled its way up her limb, cascading into the rest of her body. Okay. Fine line between pleasure and pain, and she was still undecided here. The prickle had an edge, but a weight was lifting. Stripping away.

And something else left with it. Tiny specks of blue drifted up into the golds and reds of the fire dragon, illuminated bright as fireflies before dulling into nonexistence.

'I think I love you, lizard,' Kira whispered.

Either Bradley was farting blue pebbles, or this was what was left of the utukku. Slimeball was sucking it out of her, slurping it up into his hulking Komodo self like venom out of a snakebite. And sweet baby Jesus, it was a good feeling. Kira slid off the bed, wobbled, got her footing, and fought the urge to punch the air. Shit, she was pumped. Sweaty but pumped. Dancing on her toes. Swearing never to complain about trivial stuff – headaches, blisters, hell, even period pain – ever again.

And she hoped to all the gods and demons and whatever else was out there that Az was getting this. That the good ju-ju was headed his way.

*Az, I'm all good. It's all good. Okay?*

No answer came, but she was high on not dying. Now there was a new and foreign feeling. Bradley released her thumb, pink tongue darting madly, lips peeling back to reveal far more jagged teeth than she'd imagined. His sides were bloating like balloons with each breath he took. The lizard coughed, and his dragon sun shadow shivered and popped. Komodo dragon fizzled out like a couple of dollar-store cake-top sparklers.

'Bradley, I don't know what the fuck you just did,' and kind of wish he'd done it sooner, hey, whatever, 'but I think I want to kiss you –'

The door to the room flew open, and a flurry of white and orange tumbled into the room. Tan Queen. Alive. Fucking alive.

'You're not dead,' Kira said. So damn dusty in this place, eyes stinging.

'Not yet. Let's go.' Leona panted like she'd just run an obstacle course. 'My illusions can only fool them so long.'

She clutched a half-empty soda bottle in one hand – filled with a pale yellow liquid – and scooped up Bradley with the other. Slimeball squeaked out something, and Leona clucked her tongue.

'We're all learning, none of us knows our limits. Do your best, it's all we can do in this moment.' She plonked Bradley onto her shoulder, where his orange spots clashed horribly with her green velour. 'Ready, girl?'

Distant voices floated into the room. A higher shrill rose over the deeper, shorter bursts of conversation. Ten dollars said Clara was headed their way with the band of guards Tamas had ordered.

'No. Not for any of this. Is Tamas still here?'

Just saying his name threw a couple of shivers up the old spine. Getting the taste of those utukku out of her mouth was going to take a while.

'Nope. Little weasel and his friends hightailed it out of here. Only reason I was able to get out of the cell was because he left the dimwits behind. None of us are ready for this, girl.' Leona brandished the soda bottle and its piss-like contents. 'Think I like doing my workings with cold chicken noodle soup? Not one little bit. It's embarrassing if I'm honest. But you work with what the Maiden delivers. You're still on your feet, and we're going to have a darn good chat about that when people aren't about to rush in here with guns. For now, do whatever you can with what the Maiden has gifted you. We all will.' She lifted the soda bottle, and before Kira could flinch, poured some of the cold soup she despised so much all over Kira's shoulder, soaking Nina's Jean Paul Gaultier shirt. That was going to stain. Handmaiden be pissed.

'What the hell?'

Leona recapped the bottle. 'Not even your preternatural reek is getting over the contents of your stomach. Which says a lot about the vomit, considering you stink about as much as Azrael ever did. Right now I don't have time for dry retching.' She turned, and with her back to Kira, she said, 'You've done good, girl. Stronger than I took you for. Keep it up and we might just get out of this alive.'

Holy crap, did the witch just lay a compliment on her? Kira went fish face, lips parting and closing as she struggled to work out if she was supposed to say something back.

'Come on, you fool,' Leona snapped. 'Move those bloody feet.'

That was a no then. Kira bolted after the witch and her beady-eyed buddy.

## Eron - 56

Eron disengaged his comms device, though his fingers still pressed to the unit lodged behind his right earlobe. He'd radioed in to the captain to report Agar's assertion that the target had been located. His leader had issued commands and directives, but only five of Captain Nex's words still echoed in his head, doing havoc to Eron's thoughts.

*The Lesser has been detained.*

Kira had been located and had newly arrived at the penthouse, then been laid in Tamas's hands, and was now at the mercy of the forces that worked through the Messenger, reduced as they may be. Azrael had remained elusive, the captain had informed Eron, but not before destroying most of the utukku Tamas commanded. Tempers flared. Anxiety bloated tensions. Though the captain would not assert it out loud, the discovery of that airborne creature, and Agar's inability to down it, had troubled him. That instance had been exacerbated by the run-in at the farmhouse, along with the discovery that Azrael was self-aware. Captain Nex and Tamas were at odds, the Messenger – showing a hitherto unseen level of fortitude – leaving the Facility despite the captain's vocal and vigorous declaration that it was unwise to do so.

Assertions and confidences had been undermined with the discovery that this world was not as devoid of the supermundanes as assumed. And the need for security and caution were escalated now.

*Dumuzi has been located,* he'd advised his leader with solemn brevity.

There had been a notable delay in reply, before, Are you certain?

The audible disbelief in Nex's words had irritated Eron almost as much as the question which lingered – ludicrous and infuriatingly enduring – on his own tongue. Here he was, at the very heart of events, delivering the penultimate prize to his god and leader, and what Eron desired most was to learn one thing: whether or not his moment of quiet rage, placing the phone in the captain's hands, had led Kira to where she was now, in the hands of one who despised her.

Eron pressed his clenched fists against his thighs, cursing at himself beneath his breath. This was no time for care of such trivialities. And trivialities they were. A demigod awaited. Eron relaxed his fists. He found himself alone in the car park that sat alongside the compact hospital building.

'*Brandis mer,*' he hissed, running to catch up to Agar. The gallu had ignored his heed to stand fast while he'd made the call to Captain Nex and was already partway up the short flight of stairs at the entrance.

Eron was forced into a jog to keep pace with Agar as he strode into the hospital's near-empty reception area. The gallu was far too preoccupied with his hunt to have noticed Eron's momentary lack of focus. In unison, they approached the front counter, where a lone security guard sipped from a coffee cup. Seated, a nurse leaned over his paperwork, face squelched with a frown, tapping a pen against the chart he studied. The guard, a grey-haired man whose complex skin wrinkling and thinning hair suggested an advanced age, stood to attention and moved to step in Agar's way.

'We weren't notified of any visitors. Where you guys from?'

Agar and Eron were supposed to be nondescript, from nowhere in particular. Eron was clad in casual attire – fitted black jeans, a button-up red-checked shirt, and a deep grey business jacket to further conceal the weaponry and ballistics armour strapped to his torso – in the ongoing and increasingly fruitless attempt to 'blend in'. But these people were sober. Clear of mind. And no amount of clothing truly concealed the finer edges to Eron's face and ears, the slenderness of his limbs, and the curves of his body. And no matter what Agar wore, in this case cargo pants and a high-necked black sweater, few would overlook the creature.

The imposing gallu offered one of his disingenuous smiles, revealing chalk-white teeth.

'We will pass you by.' Agar's voice grated over Eron's raw senses, but the guard didn't so much as blink. Agar pressed a chunky hand to the man's shoulder, and the guard stepped aside, gesturing to a set of double doors off to the right.

'That's the quarantined area. Right through there.'

Behind the counter, the nurse frowned at them over the rim of steel-framed glasses. 'Do they have ID?' he said, standing. 'You can't just let anyone in there.'

'All good, Mike.' The guard waved off the nurse's concerns. 'They can go through.'

Mike was clearly not so sure. His gaze swept up and down Eron's frame. But if he was perturbed by any differences he noted there, it did not show, his expression remaining tight and unreadable. The mea stone's energy pulsed, and Eron tensed. Surely, Agar did not intend to tear his way through this place. Not until they had Dumuzi, at least. After that, Eron had no regard for how the gallu sought to quench his appetite, but the feast would not begin here. Not now. Nothing would go awry with this, their victorious moment.

Fixing his inward gaze on the Bind, gathering up plentiful servings of self-loathing, Eron wrenched on the connection. Agar's head swivelled towards him, and there it was again: the smile that had once felt as though it could strip the flesh from Eron's bones. Not so now. Now it sent his pulses into uneven rhythms and his life fluid racing around his body. What pure pleasure it must be to allow oneself to drown in that utter abandon, to forsake everything of consequence and care nothing for the life surrounding you. Or those living it. Eron glanced away, recalling the earlier taste of such freedom: that moment on arrival when Agar had attacked the female and drove his blade wings deep into her body. The lust which brightened Agar also illuminated Eron's world and pushed the tedium of care and concern into the shadows where no ludicrous, enduring thoughts weighed him down.

'Be done with this. Move on.' His growl was directed as much towards Agar as to the odd chill that sought to drown him. The gallu's smile did not lower, and the tug of war on the Bind held steady. An impasse. Mike's unease grew more apparent. 'Agar, I said be done with this.'

Eron's breath came faster, harder. He braced against the Bind, readying himself for whatever Agar prepared to level at him. But it was unnecessary. Drawing closer to Mike, Agar placed his hand over the human's umber flesh and took hold of his mind quicker than one of the man's rapid heartbeats.

'Sure, go on then.' Mike nodded in that slow fashion that took them when under Agar's influence. 'Head through that door there. I'll buzz you through.'

True to his word, the man opened the wide white doors, which clicked and hummed and allowed them passage into a long corridor. An empty cart sat to their right. On the wall above hung posters about hygiene and the necessity to use antibacterial washes at all times. None of those instructions would assist anyone here. Not anymore. Human medics would struggle to cure what ailed the sick within these walls.

'Dumuzi will not ail. Are you certain you sense him?' Eron said.

'Yes.' Agar's reply was more hiss than formed word. His pace quickened.

A human padded up the hallway towards them, their sex hidden by the full bodysuit of pale blue they wore. Agar passed them by, brushing a hand against their shoulder as he went, stifling the words that had begun to fall from their lips. A woman, Eron saw now as he, too, passed her by. Her face bore traces of confusion as she stared at them from behind a panel of clear plastic. Eron hesitated, sensing she might protest. But then her gaze drifted back down to the clipboard she clung to and she continued on. When they encountered a second human, a stout man whose blue bodysuit clung hard to his ample shape, Agar was not so subtle.

'Sorry, you can't be back here without—'

The man's instructions were interrupted by the heel of Agar's hand to his forehead. The plump body stiffened, and the man's eyes widened to show complete white around irises of brown. Eron shuddered with the low pulse that moved through the Bind. Emanating from Agar, the subtle euphoria was not entirely unpleasant. He breathed into the sensation, watching the man's legs buckle, and his life end.

'Deal with this.' Agar jerked a hand towards the body at his feet before continuing on down the hall. 'We are close.'

With his exit came the evaporation of the bliss echoing down the mea stone connection. Its removal left a hollow in Eron's gut. He moved quickly, dragging the body into the nearest room. Hiding his ample body was next to impossible, and with limited time available to him, Eron decided on simply propping him in a chair beside one of the beds. A thin trickle of blood ran from the man's nose. Eron moved to turn away, but a compulsion gripped him. He ran his fingers through the crimson fluid. It glistened against his fingertips. Before he knew what he was doing, he had lifted those same fingertips to his mouth, tongue pressing against the liquid. Tangy, sharp, and utterly fixating. Eron sucked on his fingers, seeking to take possession of every drop available to him. A harsh jolt coursed through the Bind. Eron staggered. His arm was aflame with the roar of Agar's power, white-hot heat that sought to melt Eron's very bones.

*Come.* Agar's command boomed through Eron's mind. *Dumuzi is found.*

Eron ran, letting his long legs stretch and the pull of the Bind guide him. He found the gallu quickly enough. Just one room down. Agar leaned over a woman, her tight black curls thick against the white pillow, her ochre skin deepened by the stark bleach of the sheets she lay on. She was surrounded by beeping, humming machinery measuring her every bodily function. Judging by the amount of tubes and wires attached to her body, she was desperately ill. Her face was hidden from Eron's view by Agar. The gallu lowered himself closer to her face and pressed his lips against hers. The beeping of the monitor disintegrated into an irregular rhythm.

'Awaken, Dumuzi. My mistress seeks you,' Agar rumbled, running his hands across her forehead.

Eron frowned. They had been through this. Dumuzi's true soul resided in his original form.

Male.

'I don't . . .'

Eron's words shrivelled and died as Agar stepped back. A small rectangular capsule atop a silver cart and nestled close to the bed, sat almost hidden by the monitoring equipment. Agar paced around the bed, the tightness and threat inherent in his posture reminding Eron of Lahar's totem, the Syranian predator, the Precon. Closing the door to the room, Eron made the short journey to stand beside the capsule. Bound in a stark-white blanket with a pale blue trim, a wrinkled face stared up at him.

'This is him?' Eron whispered, struggling to conceal the incredulity in his tone.

There was no reply save for the rapid patterned beat of the woman's monitoring equipment. Tiny pink lips opened, and toothless gums were exposed.

Agar's hand snaked towards the child, moving with a slow, menacing pace towards the delicate, fine fingers that tugged free of the blanket. The gallu traced a finger over the honey skin of the child lying before them. His digit dwarfed the minute face, the bump of his nose, the tiny pink slash of his lips, and the two round blue orbs held wide-eyed.

'Dumuzi is an infant.' The answer was entirely obvious, but Eron desired to hear the words out loud to comprehend them.

'And it is at moments of death and birth that the demigod's true soul glows brightest.' Agar's gaze didn't leave the child. 'The goddess has been fortunate. The touch of such brightness heeded my call with haste.'

'And there is no doubt?'

The gallu's lips curled back, his brutal face hardening. 'This is the soul we imprisoned. Let me show you.'

One hand still touching the child, he whipped the other towards Eron, planting steel-strength fingertips hard against his temples. Eron cried out. An overload of sensory signals – taste, sight, touch, sound, and smell – assaulted him; every tastebud filled, his vision blurred with images, his skin pressed taut, his ears battered by a roar of sound, and his nose overwhelmed by a cavalcade of scents. His body trembled like jelly beneath Agar's touch.

'Stop!' Eron roared through the chaos, his fury lodging in the Bind and anchoring him, giving him purchase to haul himself from Agar's grip. He balled up his fist and swung. The punch landed hard enough to wipe the smirk from Agar's unkind visage. And Eron was rewarded with the faintest hint of surprise on the gallu's face. 'Enough. Send word to your kind. Assemble them here.'

The rage bubbled in his chest. Not sated.

'They already approach.' Agar touched at the place where Eron's fist had met his jaw, the smirk returning. 'Do you wish to land another blow?'

Eron bit at the inside of his cheek. It was hard to think of anything else. Even now he struggled to keep his eyes from the helpless woman in the bed. Vicious thoughts urged him to move his rage to her. The thirst for it, the bloodlust and chaos, was breathtaking. If he did not remain resolute, the Bind would suck him into an abyss he could not climb out from. But his resolution was chipped and fractured. And he was no longer certain he cared. Eron turned his back on the gallu, fighting to gather himself. He pressed shaking fingers to the comms device and placed the call to the captain.

Short and sharp: 'Dumuzi is in my possession.'

A pause, a deep intake of breath, and the captain acknowledged Eron's message. 'It seems redemption has truly found you, Eron.'

Eron disconnected the call without reply, watching the babe jerk its tiny hands at thin air. For all intents and purposes, it looked as though Dumuzi fought them even now and protested his fate. Reaching into the capsule, Eron gathered up the delicate bundle. The infant was skin and bone, impossibly fragile. It seemed incapable of withstanding what was to come. On return to the Facility, a cleansing ceremony would begin. The gods would strip away the many layers of lives that protected the prize at the child's core: the true soul of Dumuzi.

The small bundle in his arms squirmed. 'We must leave,' Eron said.

Agar's laughter rocked the room, cracking like an ice cube in a glass. *Surely, we deserve a moment to indulge, Eron?*

The Bind came alive with rough, coarse energy. Eron staggered against the bed, the child mewling in his arms.

*Sate your thirst here. This body has been engorged by the divinity that grew within. Taste.*

Agar struck like a serpent on a mouse. He clamped a square jaw around the woman's emaciated neck. Whatever illness had befallen her, it had wasted her body. Agar's head jerked in short, frantic motions, and for a moment Eron thought he might tear her throat free entirely. Blood streamed in dark ribbons across her skin, staining the white sheets beneath her. There was part of him that abhorred the ferocity, but a far greater section ached at the sight of the terrible damage. And longed to inflict it himself. Eron's throat, dry and tight with desire, did not allow his breath to come easily. A desire magnified beyond what had struck him earlier with the guard in the grounds. This lust curled like white heat through his body, joining with the feverish flow of Agar's own that seeped through the Bind.

Agar straightened, mouth a dark, moist hole of blood.

*You will not partake?* He smirked, wiping a broad hand across the mess upon his face, smearing it along his cheek. *The blood in these veins will ignite your insipid soul, god-soldier.*

Their eyes met; Eron's pulses grew rapid. The abyss widened its jaws, urging Eron closer, dangling Agar's bloody intentions before him. And Eron could resist it no longer. He stepped forward, eager, lost, and longing. The child cradled in his arms hiccupped and spewed out a tiny, fragile cry.

Eron turned away from the darkness reaching up through the Bind, the weak cry leading him clear.

'Let us go.' How raspy and broken his voice sounded, even to his own ears. Agar's head lowered, hiding the smirk Eron knew to be there.

'What are you doing in here?' A man stood in the doorway, clad in the same blue bodysuit as the other unfortunates. He gestured down the hallway. 'Can I get some help in Room 21? Get security.'

Heat shivered through the Bind, and the gallu gestured to the floor-to-ceiling window. Glass shattered. Most of it fell to the ground with an oddly musical sound, but an array of shards remained hovering in the air, catching the light as they moved. Agar stood as a conductor of a brutal orchestra. He reached one hand towards the human, and a shard darted forward, embedding itself in the man's throat. When a second human appeared, he shared a similar fate, gurgling and jerking and dying in a spreading puddle of deep red. A wheedling alarm rang out through the corridors.

Pressing the child close, Eron said, 'Do as you must, then come.'

He stepped through the empty pane, bending to avoid a dagger still clinging to the framework. Agar's fervour hummed through him, taunted him as the screams of the humans rang out in one brutal, beautiful chorus. Eron ran, as desperate to outpace his own thoughts as he was any human who still lived to pursue him.

## Kira - 57

Kira and Leona, with Bradley clinging to her shoulder,
managed only three steps down a wide hallway before the corridor
filled with a bunch of guards, much shouting, and several raised
semiautomatics.

'Shit.' Kira pressed against the wall, the fist-pump moment
giving way to shaky legs and churning guts. Her armpits dampened
with sweat, which combined with the chicken soup staining her
shirt to give her a very special perfume. She glanced at the way
they'd just come. Not much to see, only the room where had Tamas
had tried to break her into pieces, and another closed door. Damn
nice tiles on the floor, though, chequered black-and-white marble

so shiny you could probably use them as mirrors to put make-up on. All they reflected right now was the bird's nest her hair had become.

'Get on your knees,' a beefy red-headed guy barked from down the hall, crouching on one knee, gun raised. Two of his buddies remained standing, aiming over his shoulder.

Kira gave them the finger. 'Fuck you.'

One thing that could be said for the tan queen, she moved quicker than a bullet train when she needed to. Leona whipped the bottle towards the assembled group as Bradley let off loud squeaks that might have been him shitting his lizardy pants or egging his buddy on. He dove off her shoulder, scrambling towards Kira just as a spray of golden droplets launched from the bottle, perfect glittering orbs that catapulted straight at Team Dickheads. They moved faster than Leona's bullet train. So quick, Kira only knew the liquid had made contact when one of the guys, the dude at the back right, was lifted off his feet and thrown down the hall, taking a hallway table and vase with him.

'Fire!' the crouching asshat shouted, and did just that.

But not before Leona's little gang of rampaging liquid dollops gathered at the nozzle of his gun. His trajectory was thrown off. Bullets sprayed up into the ceiling, raining plaster and glass down from the overhead lights. The gun was wrenched from his hands, and the weapon propelled itself at the third dude, whose eyes couldn't have gotten any wider if he'd held them open. But they closed pretty quickly when the butt of the gun found a bullseye in the middle of his forehead.

'Jesus.'

Kira sank down to the ground behind Leona, and Bradley scrambled up onto her metal shoulder chittering like a reporter giving a play-by-play. The witch was on fire. Not literally. Which was a good thing. But she was well into the act, throwing her whole body into her movements, hands weaving in the air in front of her, hairclips bouncing round like backup dancers to one hell of a weird show. It was both fucking fantastic and terrifying to learn just what you could do with noodle soup. And she wasn't done.

Crouching-man became Flat-on-his-back-man as droplets rained down on him, hard as hail. He screamed once and then lay still. A couple of noodles stuck to his cheeks.

'Everyone all right?' Leona panted, keeping her gaze locked on the far end of the corridor.

'That was fucking amazeballs.' Kira used the wall to get to her feet.

'Not bad, huh?' Leona turned and grinned at her audience. Right when the show went into the second act.

'Shit, look out!' Kira cried.

Two more people, a man and a woman, appeared at the far end of the corridor. Only one held a gun, and both wore gobsmacked expressions as they stared at the scattered bodies.

Leona groaned and shook the bottle. Barely a sip of liquid remained. 'Damn, I shouldn't have eaten so much soup. Well, this is going to have to do. Kira, grab one of the guns.'

'A gun?' Kira shook her head. 'Are you fucking kidding?'

Leona didn't say. She was too busy pimping her soup. With a dramatic flourish, she thrust the bottle towards the couple, and a single bubble of liquid – the size of Leona's head – formed in the air before her. It barrelled towards the pair. Bullets glanced off its surface as the freckle-faced guy with the gun let off a round. Contact was a moment later. But instead of popping on impact, the bubble engulfed their upper bodies. The woman squealed and swatted at the air around her as though the bubble were a swarm of bugs. The guy clawed at his eyes, hunching over, choked sounds coming from him.

'Right, Bradley, I'm all done,' Leona declared. 'Do you have anything?'

Did the lizard have what? A sawed-off shot gun? Taser maybe? The squawk that came from his wide black mouth would have made his lizard mother proud, but it nearly deafened Kira. She slapped her hand against her ears, and Bradley dropped from her shoulder.

'Kira, stay down!' Leona shouted. 'Now, Bradley, go.'

A little rocket of onyx and orange shot down the corridor. Slimeball scrambled over two of the fallen bodies, reaching open ground just as the hallway went supernova. A goddamn star exploded, right there in the hall. Kira shaded her eyes, blinking madly. The world drew back into focus and was alive with plumes of ruby red and sun-kissed gold. Holy Christ on a cracker. It hadn't been her fucked-up brain deceiving her before when Tamas had gone all KGB on her, pumping her with god knows what. Bradley was doing it again, bringing out his super-lizard-hero self. The Komodo king was alive and well and taking up the whole damn corridor. Above the insignificant blob on white marble tile that was Bradley, the shimmering shadow of a great wide dragon head swung side to side as powerful claws edged the massive body forward. The tail, thick as a plank, thrashed from wall to wall, but not a mark appeared in the plasterwork.

Reinforcements arrived: two woman shouting and bellowing at them to stop. Both were armed because that's how they rolled here. A gun for every girl and boy.

'Stay where you are. Put your hands up.' Short-haired and deep-voiced, the woman was almost as solid as Rossiter.

Put your fucking hands up, Mr Dragon? Seriously? 'Are they insane?' Kira shouted.

'They don't see him.' Leona grabbed Kira's hand, pulling her along. 'But I think they are about to feel him.'

Bradley pulled back his teeny shoulders, and his Komodo-shadow-self did the same. Golden sides inflated with a breath before a torrent of white-hot flame poured from a mouth wide enough to swallow the dimwits who kept on coming. The explosion of heat lifted the women off their feet, arms flailing, mouths open, but not a sound escaped them.

No screaming or shouting. Just the thunk-thunk of bodies hitting walls, furniture, whatever it was that stopped their trajectory. Leona tugged Kira forward.

'Focus, girl. Focus!' she shouted.

Kira stepped over one body, then another. Everyone was drenched, as though some major-ass pool party had just gone horribly wrong. It might have been noodle soup or pure sweat from the firestorm Bradley's bigger self had just unleashed. Either way, it wasn't pleasant. Jesus. 'This is my first massacre. It's kind of distracting.'

These asshats had just shot at her, but still. Frying them all seemed extreme.

'They're not dead,' Leona said. 'I'm not a lunatic.'

Jury was out on that one. But one of the downed women groaned. Nice timing. The witch spoke truth.

Bradley lumbered his shimmering flame body along, reaching the room at the end of the hallway. Mini dragon Bradley scampered up onto a glass coffee table. Leona, still clutching Kira's hand, pulled them both into a jog, and they too reached the room. The place looked more like the penthouse in Beleiro than Tamas's digs back at the Facility. The guy was a minimalist, amongst other things, and the miniature chandelier that hung at the centre of this room probably would have made him puke. This was gaudy and way too 'look at me' for a guy who was scared of his own shadow.

Well, had been scared of his own shadow. She didn't recognise the son of a bitch that had stood over her watching her squirm. As much as she hated to admit it, that guy had scared the shit out of her. Thankfully, not literally.

'That's all they had?' Leona sniffed the air as though she could smell oncoming attacks somehow.

At the same time, Bradley's flame-throwing alter ego snuffed out, quick as any candle, and the lizard was back to his unattractive orange-and-black self splayed out on the glass like a frog on a dissection table. He barked, a six-packs-a-day kind of sound.

Kira looked to Leona. 'Well?'

'He can't hold that form anymore. He's done.' She glanced at Kira's metal arm. 'Whatever boost you gave him has run its course.'

'Me?'

'You. When did that metal start growing?'

Kira tugged up the collar of her shirt. 'How did you –'

'I'm not damn blind, girl.' Leona planted her hands on her hips. 'We really need to talk.'

But chitchat over a red wine would have to wait.

'I'd like you to stay exactly where you are, please.'

Kira spun round. The Taser-wielding bitch who had nailed her in the car, and threatened Blake, stood on the far side of the room. Clara. Dressed up as though she were about to wheel and deal at a Wall Street board meeting. An archery board apparently. She held a slender bow, silver with what looked like rubies in each tip. And if the matte-grey surface of the weapon – the way it didn't reflect the glittering light thrown by the chandelier – hadn't already screamed *I'm Telteriun!*, then Kira would have recognised it anyway. She'd managed to get Eron to go down on her once in the vault where all the Syranian goodies were kept. Fuck. Talk about places you'd rather be.

All of a sudden, Leona was up in her face. 'Kira, run, girl,' she hissed, and then bolted at Clara.

The woman raised the bow, and a thread of cobalt illuminated its length, the ruby points switching to onyx.

'Leona, no!' Kira shouted. What the fuck was the witch thinking? She was out of soup.

Apparently, Kira could move just as quickly as Leona when she wanted. One moment she was on one side of the room, the next she was throwing herself between the kamikaze witch and the Wall Street princess.

The entire room was drenched in cobalt as the bow fired.

'Fuck.' Kira threw up the armadillo, using her free arm to sling around Leona and send them both crashing to the floor. A jolt the size of Texas ran through her body, and her metal arm flung back at her. She slapped herself in the face. Not pleasant when you were made of alien steel, but nothing compared to being at the receiving end of the ricochet. Which was exactly where Clara found herself.

The bolt, a blazing cobalt arrow, shot back at her. Impact was right to the guts. Clara hit the wall and kept on going. Straight through the plasterwork.

'Oh Jesus.' Kira rolled off Leona and onto her knees. 'That's gonna hurt like hell.'

Her own cheek smarted where her metal knuckles had rebounded, but otherwise, right as rain. Armadillo intact.

'I told you to run.' Leona scrambled on all fours to the coffee table and grabbed Bradley.

'I hate funerals.' Kira staggered to her feet. Right about now any normal heart would be pounding like a freight train. But nope. The chunk in her chest could have melted for all she felt.

'I could have handled her.' Leona lowered Bradley into one of the multiple pockets on her tracksuit. If the lizard had been feeling average before, he was in for all worlds of hurt now. Sinking into a sea of gut-wrenching lime-green material would take it out of anyone, reptile or otherwise. 'You need to take care of yourself.' Leona patted her bulging pocket.

Kira shrugged. 'Me or the lizard?'

'Both. Now move.'

Just beyond the coffee table, the bow lay on the black-and-white tiles, lights extinguished. 'Wait a second.' Kira trotted on unsteady legs and snatched up the weapon. 'You've got your bubbles of power; Bradley's got the dragon thing; I get this.'

Either Clara was smaller than she seemed or the thing had shortened, retracted in on itself. It was now no bigger than a standard ruler and much lighter than Kira had expected. Might as well have been a piece of carbon fibre. Close up, the etchings in the surface were clear: Syranian lettering. And it got real dusty in the room again. Not just because Eron had been so incredible at giving head, but because maybe, just maybe, Blake was . . .

'Give me your hand.' Leona flicked her fingers at Kira. 'I need contact for the indifference workings.'

Kira did as she was told and shoved bad sister thoughts into the shitty dark hole they'd climbed out of. They hurried to a set of elevator doors just beyond the door that Clara and all her tricky happy buddies had come through. The apartment was quiet as a tomb.

'Where did everyone go?' Kira said. 'You said Tamas bolted out of here.'

Which was odd considering his hard-on for finding Az and making her life hell. She shoved the bow into the waist of her jeans and pulled her shirt over the top of it. The metal felt pleasantly warm against her skin.

'That's what bothers me. It has to be something darn important to leave us here with this lot.' Leona jabbed her fingers against the call button way too many times. Her fake nail lasted three pushes before it tinkled to the floor. 'But we'll have to assume someone sent out an SOS. We won't be alone for much longer.'

Elevator arrived, complete with inane music playing. One hundred and twenty-five storeys later, they were in the foyer. For the second time in a week, Leona kept prying eyes averted, her indifference incantation streaming from her lips in a low mutter, no one so much as glancing at them as they hurried out the main doors. Kira couldn't see her own reflection, but Leona's mandarin-coloured skin was still showing hints of fairy-floss pink from the Bradley furnace, and her hair was plastered to her forehead.

They ran out onto a sidewalk lit by streetlamps that looked like something dragged out of a Charles Dickens story. The ones in front of the building had potted plants hanging off short poles jutting from either side of the glass-encased bulbs. What time was it anyway? Not too many people around; in fact, aside from a homeless guy in the doorway across the street and a couple strolling hand in hand right by him, pretending he wasn't there, the street was empty. The shit storm in the penthouse seemed like some messed-up dream now that they were back in the real world. And in the real world, Kira needed a jacket. The air held a crispness that easily slipped through her shirt.

They chose a random direction. Left seemed good.

'Now what?' Kira broke into a graceless mix of skip and jog. 'Take a cab? Where are we going exactly? You got any witchy mates in this city?' Freedom was great, but what the fuck did they do with it?

Leona huffed and puffed, trying to match Kira's stride. 'No. The Disciples tend to stay out of the big cities. They are too far from the Maiden's heart.'

Kira left that one alone. She didn't want to talk about the goddamn Maiden right now. Or her heart.

'Where is Vail?' Leona said, quite breathless now. The Disciples needed to work on their cardio. 'Have you seen him?'

Oh, okay. It wasn't breathlessness so much as choking up. 'Good as gold,' Kira said. 'He's . . . yeah, he's all good.'

They hit the top of a side street, and Kira paused to check for oncoming traffic. Avoiding the needle-point gaze Leona was directing her way.

'And your angel?' The witch poked a little more.

'He's a million miles from here. And he's not mine, and he's not a goddamn angel.'

The last thing Kira's mind had screamed at Az was Stay the fuck away! Looks like he'd listened. And if he was doing what he was told, finding Blake and Nina, then hells to the yeah. But shit, if he came soaring in here on those pretty wings of his right now, she would start blubbering like a baby. Tamas, and what he'd done to her, was an open sore. And it was festering.

'Kira! Kira Beckworth! Shit, bro. Told you if we waited long enough, we'd hit jackpot.'

So much for keeping things on the down low. Two guys stood farther down the side road, waving at her. A redhead in a denim jacket, and a blond in a Vans sweatshirt, beaming smiles on their faces. The redhead lifted his phone to take a picture.

'No fucking pictures.' Kira ran at him, reaching for the device. 'Jesus. Privacy is a thing.'

The blond slapped down his mate's hand. They couldn't have been more than eighteen, both wore glasses, both needed haircuts, and the redhead had an enormous ring in his right earlobe. The type that stretched your skin permanently. Looking at it not only made her skin crawl – but also stirred a faint sense of recognition.

'Sorry, Kira. So sorry. Brian is a dick sometimes like that .' Non-Brian was blushing, patches that dotted his acne-ridden neck. His brown eyes kept darting between her metal hand and Leona, who still stood a little way up the sidewalk. 'We've just been . . . we were just . . . well, I just got to say I think you're awesome, but we're big fans . . . of your sister, I mean . . .' He cleared his throat.

Yeah well, he might not have been fan-boying over Blake if he knew what a fucking mess she'd made. And was in.

'You just need to piss off.'

Kira moved to walk away, but the car parked behind Brian caught her eye. Well, not so much the car but the Hello Kitty plush toy hanging from the rearview mirror. Holy fuck. Where had she seen that before?

'That your car?'

Non-Brian gave it an absent glance. 'Yeah, yeah. Hey, umm . . .is everything okay, at the Facility? I mean with the explosion, and then my sister's pilot buddies told her there had been all these helicopter flights coming here, New Weston. That's why we're here.' He pointed up at the building Kira had just run out of. 'And I don't wanna be rude, but . . . well, we saw you guys bolt out of that building, Kira. You look like hell.'

The comment slid by; Kira was too preoccupied by the redhead to bother telling Acne-boy what he could do with his rudeness. Then bingo, there it was.

'Smoking gun!' she said, in much the same way she would have actually said bingo!

Holy shit. That's where she knew the redhead from. From some grainy, shaky footage of the Facility fire that had been posted on the conspiracy-theory-nutjob website, way back when she, Leona, Vail, and Az had been sardines in the blue shitbox.

Non-Brian's eyes nearly bugged out of his head. 'Oh holy crap, you follow my site?'

'No dip –' She caught herself, turning to the redhead. 'What's your name?'

'Jared.' Jared was about to poop his pants or blow an eyeball. How did skin go that red and not burst open?

'Righto. I tell you what, I can give you an exclusive that will make you cum so hard your eyes will bleed if you help me out right now.' She could hear Leona tut-tutting, but it wasn't her reaction Kira was counting on. If she played this right, they had just struck fucking gold. And since Jared gaped as though he'd already lost a load, and Brian's neck veins were set to pop, it was gold, gold, gold. 'You said your sister's a pilot? Tell me she's here somewhere in New Weston.'

Deer-in-headlights time. 'Oh no, sorry. She's about three hours from here.'

Fuck. For once, something could have gone Kira's way.

Jared swallowed so hard his Adam's apple seemed to hit his chin. 'But her girlfriend is. She works at Essendon Airport, about an hour out. It's a small one, mainly corporate stuff over by –'

'I don't need the Wikipedia entry.' Kira strode to the car, gesturing for Leona to follow. 'Make it happen, and I'll make it worth your while. Take us to the airport.'

'Holy fuck.' Brian tore the keys from his pocket and dropped them. Jared leaned down to grab them, and they ended up butting heads.

'Jesus.' Kira got into the car, a pale yellow VW Polo that smelt surprisingly fresh inside. Leona didn't need to be told twice, coming in right after her and slamming the door hard.

'Going to share your plans?'

'Not yet,' Kira said. She wasn't in the mood for being told no right now.

Tweedledee and Tweedledum both jumped into the car, Brian in the driver's seat.

Kira made introductions. 'Smoking Gun nutjobs, this is Leona. Leona, Smoking Gun nutjobs.'

The guys exchanged a glance, smirking.

'So awesome,' Brian said.

'Kira Beckworth is in our car, man.'

'Oh for fuck's sake,' Kira said. But only under her breath. Too damn wiped to be more vocal. And besides, if she filled their wet dreams, it meant it would be a hell of a lot easier to get them to do what she wanted. And so far, they were off to a good start.

The car jiggled and rumbled to life, and they pulled out into the intersection. Brian watched Kira in the rearview as he waited for a slow-moving semi-trailer to pass before he could turn.

'Can you tell us anything now, Kira? I mean, the riots, and the outbreaks. Does the Facility have something to do with all that?'

'Outbreaks?' Okay, she'd bite.

Jared turned in his seat, eyes bright. 'The government is keeping it under wraps so the city doesn't go totally insane. Saying there is some flu going around. But we're hearing that there are centres out of town, quarantine zones, that are dealing with some kind of superbug. Come on, Kira. There's a link, right? I mean the Facility has an explosion big enough to register on the Richter, then they have aircraft going in and out of New Weston, and Tamas Cressly is rumoured to be in town. Shit must be real bad. Did the Facility lose control of a contagion here?'

Brian joined the conspiracy-fest, but kept his eyes on the road. 'Did they lose the aliens? They lost the aliens, right? And they are the ones spreading the virus?'

Kira went all out to keep her expression neutral, but inside it was a free-for-all. Quarantine zones? Sweet fucking Jesus, what was going on? Her ribs knit together and wouldn't let her take a deep breath. She didn't realise she was clenching her flesh hand until Leona placed hers over it. Tan queen's touch was warm, as if she'd just stepped out of her sunbed. Or maybe Kira was as cold on the outside as she felt inside.

'Slow and steady, Kira,' Leona said, so gentle it just made things worse.

A knot the size of a walnut lodged itself in Kira's throat. Slow and steady wouldn't help Blake. *Christ, B. Don't be dead. For fuck's sake, don't be dead.* A screwed-up relationship was better than none.

Brian pulled to a stop at a red light. They were the only car on the road. 'What happened in there, Kira?' He licked his lips and continued when Kira didn't answer. 'Are they . . . were they trying to . . . to program you to do something you didn't want to do? Did they try to add more parts or something?'

That one just wouldn't die. Kira the android. Fuck, if only. If she were a robot, someone could switch her off. Make her brain stop hurting.

Brian wasn't done, despite Kira's death stare. He nodded at her in the mirror. 'Your neck, that's new right? Is this old lady helping you escape the Facility? Have you malfunctioned or something?'

Maybe she had. Anyone in their right mind *would* be attempting to escape the Facility. Not planning to haul their ass back there.

'Oh Brian, man,' Jared moaned. 'Not cool.'

'That's enough.' School Principal Leona's words were hard as a ruler on knuckles. 'Mind your manners, or I'll make you fart rodents and sneeze gnats.'

'What? I was just asking!' Brian cried. 'How could I fart rodents?'

'Would you like me to give you a demonstration?' Leona raised her hands and was met with a chorus of 'Please don't,' 'I'm sorry,' and 'She's crazy, man.'

For once, the only one silent, with nothing whatsoever to say, was Kira.

# Eron - 58

Eron used his elbows to nudge aside the shrubbery, hunching his shoulders at the hum of abandon that moved through the Bind. For now, he would allow Agar close to free rein. There was little point in concealing the gallu's presence; the hospital was too coated in blood to ignore it. So Eron would use Agar as a distraction to ensure his own undetected departure from the grounds. In time he would summon the gallu to return to his side.

It was not an entirely selfless plan. Greater distance from the most powerful of the Four would enable Eron time to reassemble his composure. But the interminable screech being issued by the baby was making that a difficult task. With each step away from the cradle where it had lain, the sound rose. Higher, and louder than before. A wrinkled face darkened with the effort of delivering such a noise, as though Dumuzi roared defiance at his fate. At this rate, it might draw more attention than Agar's rampage.

Added to Eron's woes, it had begun to rain, a light smattering but irksome nonetheless. The landscape beyond the manicured grounds around the hospital was thick with trees and ground cover, and now he was beyond the artificial lighting that illuminated the building's immediate vicinity. The journey was far more encumbering than he'd first imagined. Several low branches had succeeded in pulling much of his hair from where it was bound at the back of his neck. Eron pressed at the comms link, issuing orders to the waiting pilot for extraction from the place she had left them barely an hour before.

'Sir, there is an approaching military aircraft en route to the hospital.' The female pilot might have been discussing the day's menu, her voice devoid of any particular concern or urgency. 'They are responding to an emergency call from the location. I have relocated to another point. Sending coordinates to you now.'

Eron's slew of Syranian and human curses didn't rise above the howl of the infant. The coordinates buzzed through, filling the screen on the watch at his wrist, activating the GPS system there and guiding him to the new location. Eron shifted the unhappy child from his left arm to his right so he could view the instructions. Within two steps his boot caught on something hidden in the foliage, and Eron almost lost his footing and the child both. Gathering himself, he shifted a piece of the blanket over the infant's face in the vain hope it might stifle or at least dull the incessant screams. He focused on the Bind and calling Agar to him.

A gust of wind played through the trees, tossing the rain and branches alike. A dark shape lowered down through the canopy. Agar, his wings unfurled but held close to his body as he negotiated the narrow space between the trees and settled on the ground up ahead. His appendages, formed of Telteriun and shaped to resemble those worn by the angels of human folklore, were actually many narrow strips of metal held close together. Snaking lengths, like a bunch of whips, connected at a point on the gallu's back where a space had been made in the body to accommodate them. The clink and clattering sound they made as they moved betrayed their metallic structure. There was some beauty in the design, beauty that was stripped from the creature they adhered to.

*Come.*

Agar reached out his arms. Eron hesitated before turning his back and allowing the gallu to embrace him, lifting them from the ground. They rose up through the trees and drew clear of the foliage. With every beat of Agar's wings, the air was pummelled by great gusts. The child fretted, screwing up his small face as rain patted against it. But he no longer bellowed. With each downward strike of Agar's wings as they moved away from the bloodshed and closer to their goal, a euphoria deepened in Eron's chest.

He held Dumuzi to his breast. He, Eron, cradled the demigod that both his god Lahar and the Queen of Kur Herself, Ereshkigal, had tasked them with sourcing. In Eron's arms, likely pressed too tightly against the hard armour beneath his clothing, lay the very reason for his anointment as a god-soldier. Eron's reason for being. And this pathetic, noisy creature would wipe away all trace of Eron's disgrace. His lips curved, a smile flirting with their edges. The tightness in his throat was no longer the burn of lust, but something far more beatific.

The child's mouth opened, and milky, lumpy liquid jerked from between toothless gums. Eron scowled, lifting the baby away from his chest, but the regurgitation had already made its mark on his shirt.

Agar tilted upright, drawing to a halt. Hovering. The gallu's grip around Eron's waist tightened, and a pulse of low, tense energy moved through the Bind.

'What is it?' Eron said. 'What do you sense?'

*We are not alone.* Agar leaned forward, and urgency to his wingbeats returned. The wind rushed through Eron's loosened hair, now heavy and damp from the increasing rain.

'Who approaches?'

The gallu gave no reply, and the throb of the Bind dissipated into a mere whisper. Agar dropped lower, skimming uncomfortably close to the branches, weaving in and out of them. Something scraped at Eron's cheek, and his foot banged hard against a branch.

He hunched himself into a ball, the child low against his belly. Agar's wings sliced their way through the foliage, leaves and narrow branches tearing free and falling behind them as he passed.

'Caution!' Eron shouted.

At this rate Dumuzi might be ripped from his grip altogether. Up ahead, the denseness of the trees evaporated. Eron caught a glimpse of the waiting helicopter, its blades spinning in a clearing just barely wide enough to accommodate it. The pilot had not landed, hovering just above the uneven ground. Agar's trajectory hastened, and he lowered them farther.

*Ready yourself. I will set you down.*

Despite his words, Agar gave Eron no time to ready himself. He and the child fell. A short distance, granted, nothing that would harm his enhanced god-soldier bones or sinew, but the shock forced a short, sharp cry from Eron's lips. In order to maintain his hold on the child, he was forced to land on his knees. The impact shuddered through him, the child's head smacking against the edged contours of Eron's body armour, and an indignant cry emitting forth from Dumuzi's mouth once again. It was lost beneath the deep hum of the helicopter's engine, a small blessing. But another greater sound was not so easily drowned out.

From right overhead came the thunderous crash of tree limbs breaking. Scrambling to his feet, Eron threw himself clear of the descending projectiles, landing hard on his side, rotting ground cover cracking beneath the press of armour. He rolled onto his knees, seeking out the source of the chaos above.

They were certainly not alone. Metal thrashed, carving through great chunks of timber, decapitating treetops and amputating branches, as Agar fought off his attacker. An adversary Eron had last viewed rising into the air with Kira bound in his arms.

Azrael.

Even from where he crouched, far below, Eron had no doubt. The gallu's wings spread in a glorious plume of metalwork far more delicate but equally as deadly as Agar's. Azrael. The creature whose return Tamas's goddess had demanded.

And whose recorded closeness with Kira had pried from Eron an acidic coil of jealousy.

During the training with the mea stones, this being had been a wretched, manipulated, tortured thing, broken time and again by the Syranians and their ministrations.

Azrael was not broken now.

Despite Agar's well-timed strikes, Azrael seemed to predict each move, sweeping in majestic turns to angle his lithe body out of range of Agar's brutal thrusts. This was not the creature they had levelled in training.

The Bind hummed with energy that stuttered and flowed in equal measure. But the sensation was distant, as though Agar held Eron at arm's length. Eron's pulses thumped with far heavier purpose. He rose to his feet, lunging into great, loping strides, crashing through the undergrowth and ignoring the tug and claw of the foliage around him. Ignoring the squeals of the child in his arms. Striving for the confines of the awaiting helicopter. The downpour hammered at the earth now. As he ran, Eron scanned his surrounds, searching through the shadows for any hint that Azrael was not alone. The helicopter's downdraft flung sodden debris into the air. Eron blinked, shielding his eyes, glancing back at the treetop battle. No sign of either gallu. Eron hauled himself and his precious cargo into the aircraft, pulling the door closed. The child screamed as if he were the one doing battle with Agar.

'Go!' Eron shouted.

But the pilot was already doing so, and the aircraft was already rising. Eron pressed fingertips against the half-moon shape implanted behind his ear. Crackling static played with the connection.

'What is your status, Eron?' Captain Nex's words bloomed as though he stood right beside Eron, his silken voice, as always, holding its acidic edge.

'Azrael.' Eron struggled to manoeuvre his seatbelt over his body one-handed, the pilot not making it any easier when she jerked the craft hard right. 'Captain, Azrael has located us. Request immediate assistance.'

Beyond the rain-smeared windows, far closer than gave Eron comfort, two shapes darted and weaved at each other. A sublime show of manoeuvrability. The two gallu fought with the grace of martial arts partners sparring, the fluidity of the movement a testament to the brilliance of Blake's designs. The Bind shuddered with each blow landed.

'Eron, do not . . .' The captain's voice fought to make its way through snapping static. ' . . . strength . . . utukku.'

The static engulfed the conversation, rending the captain's directives incomprehensible.

'Captain? Captain Nex?' Eron pressed at the comms device, as though doing so would improve its function. It did not. And though it was clear the captain still attempted communications, there was no deciphering his words.

The pilot dropped altitude with gut-churning rapidity. Agar and Azrael shifted dangerously close to the aircraft. Eron pressed against the window, bouncing the restless infant in his arms and watching as Azrael landed a pounding blow to Agar's midriff with a high kick. Now the vibration running through the Bind lifted, an unpleasant sensation of movement within the mea stone embedded in Eron's arm. He frowned, his reflection in the glass revealing an unkempt and concerned appearance. Azrael arched back, just out of reach of Agar's violent return parry, a strike with the furthermost tip of his left wing. But the move met only empty air, and Agar tilted off balance, his bulk threatening to send him in a full rotation. In that uncertain moment, Azrael moved in and flung a glancing blow against Agar's torso. Searing knife blades of energy ricocheted through the Bind. Eron let out a choked cry, and the child startled in his arms, set off afresh with new tears.

But Agar was not felled, and his black rage flooded Eron's senses. The mightiest of the Four snaked out of reach of every thrust and dive Azrael levelled at him. And all the while they followed along the helicopter's path, never moving more than a few meters beyond its rotating blade, no matter the pilot's attempts to shift them out of range. She turned in her seat, shouting at him. Eron grabbed the headset from where it still rested on a hook beside his seat, shoving it over his head.

'Sir, what would you have me do?' Briefly Eron wondered where else this woman had flown to enable such calm in her tone.

'Stay in the air. Continue course to the Facility as instructed. No deviation.'

Eron shouted instructions, his eyes never once leaving the display beyond the window. Azrael used his wing tips like daggers against his opponent, dodging Agar's own attempts to impale him. He laid several precise punches, sending Agar recoiling. Each hit pounded through the Bind, not exactly painful, but Agar's usual animal-like fierceness was tempered with the heavy weight of concentration. Agar wasn't taking any chances. Eron gave him full rein, his bones aching as the mea stone clung to the very smallest of links with the gallu. Agar shot high into the air, Eron straining his neck to try to follow the gallu's path, before the gallu dropped straight down. This time behind Azrael, who seemed to have been caught off guard by the sudden movement. Thrusting both wing tips forward, Agar slammed them into Azrael's back.

Despite himself, Eron gasped. 'Direct hit,' he whispered to no one in particular.

Agar wrenched his wing tips free, darting in to wrap an arm around Azrael's neck. The gallu hung limp in the arms of one of the Four, no sign of fight left. The pair rotated in the air, and Eron caught a glimpse of a subdued golden glow emanating from Azrael's back. The Telteriun carapace, the cage designed to ensure the unearthly beings longevity in this world, had been punctured. How long could the creature survive with such damage? Indeed, did it mean a death sentence for Azrael? There had been no instruction to destroy the escaped gallu. The opposite in fact. The goddess had made it clear She wished to see Her property returned in working order.

Azrael's torn shirt revealed great gashes in the faux skin across his chest, though these had not penetrated the Telteriun. Agar, too, had pieces of skin hanging at his shoulders, clothing stripped away. But he was far from done.

Agar tilted Azrael's head and stretched a wing, readying to strike again.

Eron dove inward for the connection, reaching for the Bind. No. Desist.

Pure, ripe rage was his answer from Agar, flooding down the Bind and thrusting Eron back against his seat. The mea stone sought to burn through his very bone. But Agar had to be denied.

*No more. Do not destroy him.* Eron dug into the connection, and his body strained against the gallu's fervour.

Agar sought to destroy, to tear the gallu he held into pieces. The darkness in his mood threatened to envelop them both. But Eron sought more than destruction; he sought irrevocable redemption. To bask in the glory of the gods. He would not only bring them Dumuzi. He would bring them Azrael.

And his fury rose to meet Agar's own. The flow of energy reversed and Eron sent torrents down the Bind, aimed at Agar's core.

*Do as I say. Descend. Bring the gallu to me.*

Eron marvelled at the force of his thoughts, the utter command in their timbre. He was master, and Agar would bend. Or the gallu would break.

This time it was Eron who pushed Agar towards that onyx pit that dwelt between them. And he was rewarded with a shiver of relenting energy finding its way through the Bind. The gallu lowered his wing and, with his prize still clutched in his arms, did as he had been told.

Eron directed the pilot to follow. Azrael could be placed in Agar's inhibitor cuffs for the journey, though the gallu hardly looked to be a threat, still showing no sign of resistance. Or indeed, life. Perhaps it was already too late, and the goddess's lost property was beyond even her divine touch now.

No matter. Eron was too buoyed by his victory over Agar, and the capture of both Dumuzi and Azrael, to hold any great concern. He exhaled, slow and calm, and sat back against his seat. In his arms, the child gazed up at him, blue fathomless eyes now dry. Pitiful cries at last, abandoned.

**Reviews are awesome!**
**I'd love to know what you think of Metal Angels.**
**If you have a moment, head to your favourite site and leave a**
**review :)**
**Amazon    *    Goodreads    *    Kobo    *    Bookbub**

**Want to keep up with all the good stuff yet to come?**
**Subscribe Now!**

daniellekgirl.com

Fantasy                    Sci-fi                    Paranormal

.